PERFECT CHRISTMAS

Kirsty Perfect adores Christmas so much that she owns an all-year-round Christmas shop. When handsome Alan Carter arrives to take over the running of the art gallery next door while his uncle is ill, could love be in the air? Meanwhile, Kirsty's sister Lara is falling under the spell of Alan's brother Ian, whose troubled son William is struggling to settle as her newest young pupil at school. And Martha and Bob Perfect are dreading their first Christmas after selling the much-loved family home . . .

CAROL MacLEAN

PERFECT CHRISTMAS

Complete and Unabridged

LINFORD
Leicester

First published in Great Britain in 2018

First Linford Edition
published 2018

A catalogue record for this book is available
from the British Library.

ISBN 978–1–4448–3751–3

Published by
F. A. Thorpe (Publishing)
Anstey, Leicestershire

Set by Words & Graphics Ltd.
Anstey, Leicestershire
Printed and bound in Great Britain by
T. J. International Ltd., Padstow, Cornwall

This book is printed on acid-free paper

1

Kirsty Perfect was making hot chocolate. Luxury hot chocolate. With extra cream and marshmallows. She shivered and pulled the rollneck of her Christmas-themed jumper snugly up towards her ears. She was standing in the tiny back room of her shop at her equally tiny worktop and sink. The little window looked out on an enclosed square. Beyond the glass, there was a steady drizzle of sleety rain. It blurred the yellow lights of the other windows opposite.

Kirsty felt another shiver, this time of excitement. What if it snowed? After all, it was only a month until Christmas. And it was her all-time favourite season. In fact, she loved Christmas so much that she owned and ran a Christmas shop that stayed open all year round.

In the cramped back room, along with her sink, worktop and trusty kettle, there was a small desk and metal office chair. On the desk, her laptop lay open. The screen saver, a cracker that burst open in a spray of coloured stars over and over again, danced madly. She stared at it briefly as if it was a wild and dangerous animal. Then she turned back to the window and sipped at her delicious hot chocolate, willing the soggy rain to turn into beautiful, white flakes of snow.

What would this Christmas be like? The Perfect family had had wonderful Christmases in the family home they called Hambly. But now Hambly was sold and Kirsty and her younger sister, Lara, had moved into flats while their parents, Bob and Martha, had bought a brand-new bungalow in a new residential area of the town. Kirsty's flat was right above her shop. It was ideal for rolling out of bed and stumbling downstairs with a mug of coffee in hand to open up. Lara seemed to like her new apartment too in the centre of the town. But the sisters knew that their parents missed Hambly.

'It's just too much work,' Bob Perfect had said firmly.

Kirsty and Lara had been asked to stay home early one Sunday evening in the middle of summer for a family conference.

'I'm not getting any younger, and neither is your mother. I can't keep up with the roof repairs and the ceiling leaks and the wonky electrics. It's an old house, and my knees can't cope with three flights of stairs anymore. Mum feels the same.'

Kirsty glanced at her mother. Martha's face showed conflicting emotions. 'Mum? Is that really what you want?' she asked.

'Dad's right,' Martha Perfect said. 'We've loved Hambly so dearly, and we'll miss it very much. But we're in our sixties now, and it's time to think about the future. A nice new bungalow will do us very well.'

Kirsty knew Mum would never argue with Dad — not in front of the children, as she used to say. She rolled her eyes at Lara. Lara smiled back.

'Are you sure you're ready to sell up?' Kirsty persisted.

She looked around her sadly. Hambly was a wonderful, rambling old brick house. The brickwork was almost covered in ivy. The windows were mullioned and the roof tiles were overlapping, like a house out of a history book. In fact, Hambly dated back to the seventeenth century. It was surrounded by a wild acre of garden where Kirsty and Lara had spent their blissful childhoods.

'Yes, we're sure, darling. Nothing you say can change our minds,' Martha said gently.

'But . . . ' Kirsty was ready to argue.

'All good things must come to an end,' Lara said quietly. There was a shininess to her blue eyes, and she sniffed and wiped her nose on a tissue.

'What a lot of tosh!' Kirsty

4

exclaimed. 'I don't believe good things must end. Why on earth should they?'

Lara shrank from her and Kirsty forced herself to relax. How different they were, she thought. Like the proverbial chalk and cheese. Kirsty was dark-haired and brown-eyed, and liked nothing more than a good argument which she dived into with gusto. Lara, two years her junior, with her fair hair and blue eyes, was shy and avoided conflict.

'Kirsty,' Martha said warningly. She hugged Lara close and kissed the top of her head.

Kirsty remembered horrible Mark and kicked herself mentally. Idiot! She had to remember that Lara was still fragile. Her engagement had been broken off only a few weeks before. 'Sorry,' she said. 'It's just . . . I can't bear to lose Hambly. It's got all our memories. Think of all the lovely birthdays and family get-togethers we've had here. And . . . our wonderful Christmases.' Her own eyes were wet.

She rubbed them savagely with her fingers. She wasn't going to cry.

Martha's arms reached to include her in a group hug. Then Bob joined them and for a long moment they all thought about their home. Then Martha said the roast was ready and they all went to the table ready for another meal. One of the last Sunday roasts in Hambly, Kirsty thought with a pang. It didn't matter what her mother might say, she wasn't convinced her parents were doing the right thing. They weren't that old, for goodness' sake. It seemed rather early to be thinking about living without stairs to climb and without a garden to tend. It was awful to imagine them not living here, in a house that Kirsty had always felt was filled with friendly ghosts and thick with history.

Bob carved the roast lamb and the delicious aromas of gravy and rosemary wafted in the warm air. Kirsty passed the potatoes and Lara served up the glazed carrots. Once they all had their plates in front of them, Martha spoke.

'Hambly must go,' she said. 'But Dad and I don't want to leave you two with nowhere to live. We'd like to help financially with you getting your own places.'

Kirsty hadn't thought about that. Losing Hambly was a terrible wrench. But where was she to live now? She frowned and then realised she had the solution easily.

'Thanks, Mum, but there's a flat above the shop,' she said. 'The previous owner used it as a junk store, but if I clear it out I can live there.'

'Are you sure?' Martha looked worried.

'Yes, it'll be fine,' Kirsty said. 'It needs a good scrub and a lick of paint. But actually, when I think about it, it makes sense. I'll be right at my place of work.'

'What about you, Lara?' Bob asked, standing up to carve some more roast. 'Where would suit you?'

'There's a couple of flats for sale off

the town square,' Lara said. 'Some-where like that would be okay. I can walk from there to the school. And I'd be very glad of some money towards it, but I'd pay you back when I can.'

'If you don't want to be on your own, you can stay with me,' Kirsty offered.

Since the whole unpleasant situation with Mark, Lara hadn't gone out much alone. She shook her head. 'Thanks, but maybe Hambly going is a sign I need to move on. The first step is independence. A flat of my own is a good start.'

Martha gave her an approving smile, and the conversation had moved on to other topics. The decisions were made, and the family always supported each other.

Now, Kirsty finished off her hot chocolate and put the mug in the sink. Her gaze was drawn once more to the laptop. Was she going to do this or not? Making a hot drink was simply a distraction. She was putting off making a decision. Taking a deep fortifying breath, she went over and sat down at the desk. She drummed her fingernails on the wooden top. Then she moved the mouse, waking the screen.

On it was a symbol of an apple tree full of blossom. 'Find your own fruitful relationship,' the brand line promised. As she clicked on the tree, the website pages opened up. It all looked so easy to do. She had to send a profile image of herself and details such as her age, hobbies and interests and so on. Her finger hovered over the highlighted link. She absolutely knew that Martha would disapprove of this. Lara would too. Her sister wouldn't dream of trying online dating in a million years. After her experiences with Mark, Kirsty didn't think Lara would date anyone again for a long while.

Stop thinking about Lara and Mum, Kirsty told herself, *and instead let's think about what I want.* The trouble was, she knew exactly what she wanted, just not how to go about getting it. Was it wrong to want to get married and have kids? She hadn't even told her friends. They saw her as an independent businesswoman and admired her for running her shop on her own. Her friends were all pursuing their careers. None of them mentioned children and homemaking. It was . . . old-fashioned and didn't fit the image they all projected. At twenty-six, she had plenty of time to meet someone and settle down. But she never met any eligible men. She lived in a small town. She wasn't working in a busy office where there might be single men.

No, Kirsty decided, she had to go after what she wanted. If she was unlikely to meet suitable men naturally, then she had to take the initiative. She pressed the link. Within minutes she had uploaded a profile picture of herself. It was a nice shot that Lara had taken on a walk in the woods. Her long dark hair looked good, and she was pretty enough. She was no beauty, but she had nice clear skin, and that had to count for something, didn't it? She added in some hobbies. She loved to paint with oils and watercolours. She adored Christmas. She liked to walk in the countryside. She typed it all in. Should she exaggerate and put skydiving? What if her date asked her to skydive with him? No, that was a mistake. She had to be honest.

But when it came to clicking on the 'Go' button, which would confirm her request to add her profile to their site, her finger hesitated. With a sigh, she put down the mouse. Was she really ready for this step? It was daunting. She might meet her soulmate; but then again, she might meet somebody like Mark.

At that moment, the bell tinkled. Someone had come into the shop. It had been a slow day, perhaps due to the dismal weather, so she was glad of a customer. She was glad, too, not to have to make the final decision just yet.

Kirsty went through into the shop. There was a lovely scent of cinnamon, cloves and oranges from the potpourri.

A real Christmas smell. Whoever had come in was hidden from sight by the wide tree she had decorated freshly in the middle of the floor. Around the sides of the shop were tall shelves full of Christmas decorations, ornaments, scented candles and leafy wreaths.

'Hello? Can I help you?' she said.

The man stepped out from behind the tree and Kirsty's breath caught in her throat. He was gorgeous. He was tall with dark gold hair and piercing blue eyes. He had the kind of strongly jutting jaw a cowboy would kill for. Broad shoulders and a lean frame completed him. She hoped she hadn't moaned out loud.

'Sorry?' she murmured.

He'd spoken but she hadn't heard a word of what he'd said. 'I'm looking for tree decorations,' he said, a slight crinkle of confusion on his forehead. Clearly he thought she was a bit odd. Kirsty smiled professionally and tried to remember she was an independent businesswoman who was very good with customers.

'Yes, of course. What sort of thing are you after? I've got lovely wooden figures just in from Germany.' There, that was better. She sounded completely normal, even if her nerves were doing a loop-the-loop.

The shop was small and cluttered, so she had to squeeze past him to get to the shelf. It made her heart flutter madly. She took down some of the wooden carvings. She loved these. Each was hand-crafted and individually painted. There were Santa Clauses, tiny people on sleighs, angels and snowmen. They were so well made, each figure's face was different. She wanted some herself. If they didn't sell, she'd take some for her flat decorations. It wasn't yet December; but once the month changed, her flat was going to be festooned in seasonal glory.

He shook his head apologetically. 'They're very nice, but I'm looking for . . . well, I think I'm meant to be getting . . . matching blue and white baubles, that sort of thing.'

'You don't sound very sure.'

'It's a blue theme, you see, this year. So the tree baubles have to be blue too. Except, apparently that's too . . . blue . . . on its own, so the white ones will complement the theme.'

'Are you shopping for someone else?' Kirsty asked.

'Yes, my girlfriend wants me to get the decorations. She's doing the rest.'

Typical. He's got a girlfriend. Of course he does. How could a gorgeous guy like him not have one?

Her nerves stopped singing and her heart went back to its usual boring beat. Just her luck. The most handsome man she'd ever met was already taken. Although why she thought he'd be interested in her anyway was arrogance on her behalf. Kirsty bit her lip. She was nothing special. Maybe that was why she was destined to be alone for the rest of her life.

'So, can you help me please?' he said hopefully.

14

She took pity on him. It wasn't his fault she'd had a mad moment of dreams about him. 'I have just the thing for you.' She smiled and led him to the other shelf. There were neat packages of uniform baubles. There were several colour ranges, and she picked up the pale blue and a snowy white set. His expression brightened.

'What a relief. I didn't want to go back empty-handed.'

The girlfriend was obviously a tyrant, Kirsty decided. It was cruel asking someone else to go shopping for specific items that you wanted. Clearly he only had a small chance of getting the right stuff. Well, she was going to make sure he did. 'You know, I've got some wonderful tinsel in these shades too. How about I get you a box?'

'Great! Is there anything else I need?'

'I have matching napkins, and I also have crackers in eggshell-blue with white tracery.'

'I'll take all that. Thanks.'

The pre-packaged baubles were Kirsty's

least favourite. There was something soulless about them. They would create a designer look to Christmas; but where were the memories, the quirkiness of individual decorations? She much preferred the tiny wooden figures. At home, the tree decorations included strange objects she and Lara had made at school and some old glass baubles that had belonged to her grandparents. But the customer was always right. Just because she liked Christmas a certain way didn't mean everyone did.

'I'm Alan Carter, by the way,' he said suddenly, thrusting out a large hand for her to shake.

'Kirsty Perfect.' His handshake was warm and firm. She ignored the tingle that shot up her arm. It was inappropriate.

'Ah, hence the shop's name — Perfect Christmas.' He grinned.

Kirsty grinned back. 'Yes, I'm lucky that I've got the perfect surname.'

He laughed. It was an old joke, well-worn in the Perfect household but

16

funny to those who hadn't heard it. She was slightly embarrassed to use it on him. But he seemed to be genuinely amused. So he was not only handsome, but nice too. She busied herself by parcelling up his purchases.

'I'm actually just next door, in the gallery,' Alan said.

'I thought it was shut. Mr Timmons hasn't been well.' In fact, she knew the gallery next door was shut. It had been for the last few weeks. She was worried about Mr Timmons. He was a friendly neighbour to her. It also wasn't good for business to have a shut shop next door, but that mattered a lot less than her old friend's health.

'Yes, Uncle Simon's had to go into hospital, unfortunately. I've come to look after the gallery until he's better.'

'Will he be all right?'

'I believe so. The doctor wants to run some tests, but he's hopeful they can treat him and that he can come home in a few weeks.'

'That's good. Please pass him my

best wishes when you visit him. It'll be nice to have the gallery opened again. Besides, this is his busy season when everyone's looking for a good Christmas present.'

Alan nodded. 'That's true. I hope I can do him proud. I've never run a gallery before.'

'If you need any help, just pop through and I'll do what I can,' Kirsty said. She gave him the parcels.

'Thanks for the offer of help, and thanks for helping me choose these. It's a bit of a minefield, buying things, isn't it? Still, I'm sure Karen will be pleased with these. I'm staying at Uncle Simon's house and we'll have Christmas there. Karen wants it to be perfect.'

He smiled as he realised he'd used the word 'perfect'. It created a dimple in one cheek and Kirsty had to look away. Did he realise he could be in the movies? She imagined him on the range with tight blue faded jeans, a checked shirt and a wide-brimmed cowboy hat. It was suddenly warmer in the shop.

'We aim to please,' she said. It was meant to be amusing but came out sounding a bit short.

'Well, I mustn't keep you,' Alan said, waving the parcels. He nodded quickly and headed to the door.

When the bell had tinkled and the door was shut, Kirsty wrinkled her nose. The shop felt really empty. The silence was overwhelming. She stomped over to her tablet and stuck on a playlist of uplifting jolly seasonal tunes. The tunes failed to please her.

Still in stomp mode, she went into the back room. She woke up the laptop. Before she could think about it any further, she hit 'send' on her application. *There.* If all the men she met in real life were in relationships, then she had to be proactive and find herself a date online!

2

The school desks were all covered in pieces of cardboard, masses of fluffy cotton-wool balls, glue and glitter. An excited hubbub of voices filled the room. Miss Perfect's primary one class were making Christmas cards. Lara smiled as she walked around, seeing the happy faces and concentrated effort with scissors and glue sticks. She helped Samantha stick a cotton-wool beard onto a jolly Santa, and Kyle to cut around a snowman silhouette. Every so often, an eager hand would shoot in the air for her attention. Four- and five-year-olds did their best, but some of them still struggled with motor skills. Although the activity looked like plain fun, there were aims and objectives carefully planned behind the lesson. There were skills to be learned and practised, but Lara believed firmly that her pupils learned best when they were happy.

It was only three weeks until the holidays, and there was a lot to be done. They were in the run-up to the school nativity, and her class was singing two special songs. Then there were the costumes to be made. Lara hoped the parents and carers would help with those. If not, she knew her mother would step in and help. Martha was a dab hand with sewing.

Lara wondered if her mum was all right. She'd popped in at the weekend to take her parents some homemade scones and found them sitting quietly in their new front room. They both seemed ill at ease, and Lara guessed they'd had an argument before she arrived. She knew they would never mention it so didn't bother to ask. Still, she was concerned about them. She'd phone Kirsty later, she decided. See if she'd noticed anything.

She made a shushing sound as the noise in the classroom reached a crescendo, and her pupils obediently tried to whisper. She was proud of her classroom control. In fact, it was only at her work that Lara felt any confidence at all these days.

Being with Mark had knocked all the stuffing out of her. She hadn't realised just how much he had dominated her life. It had been a whirlwind romance, and he'd proposed only three weeks after they'd met on a Mediterranean cruise. She'd been so enthralled by him and flattered by his close attention to her that she'd said yes. What a mistake. His attention had turned out to be a form of control. In the two years of their engagement, it had got worse and worse.

He didn't like her going out with friends. He disliked what she wore. He didn't like her family. He refused to visit Hambly; instead, she had to visit his house out of town. Luckily, they had never moved in together. She'd wanted to wait until they were married. In return, Mark had pressurised her to move the wedding forward. Some instinct had made her refuse. Partly, she didn't want to deprive Martha and Kirsty of the fun of wedding planning. But maybe some deep-down part of her had known, even then, that there was something wrong. Lara hoped so. She wanted to believe that her instincts were right at some level. Because she had now lost any trust in people, and in her own judgement. The man who was supposed to be the love of her life had turned out to be a bully. And she had chosen him. What did that say about her? She knew she'd never be able to meet anyone else. She'd always worry that they'd change and become like Mark.

The worst part of it was that he wouldn't leave her alone. He phoned her and texted her until she changed her phone number, and also tried to visit her. Or he'd bump into her in town as if by coincidence. Twice he'd asked her to go back to him and she'd told him no. Now he'd taken to waiting for her outside the school occasionally. If she wished to, she could pull up the blinds right now and see him lounging next to the school railings.

Lara tried to block her dark musings. She smiled brightly as she asked the children to start tidying up. It was time for the next lesson, one that everybody liked, which was storytelling.

The door opened and the head teacher, Moira Mellon, came in. She had a small boy by the hand. 'Lara, I've got a new pupil for you. This is William, who has just moved to our town. William, this is your new teacher, Miss Perfect.'

Lara crouched down to the boy's level. 'Hello, William. How are you? Do you want to come and join in with the class?'

He nodded shyly. Lara took him over to an empty chair and told him that was his place. She put some paper and pencils in front of him so he could draw while she went back to the head teacher.

'He doesn't say much,' Moira whispered to her. 'I hope he fits in okay.'

Lara looked over to where the blond head was bent over the paper drawing. 'I'm sure he'll be fine. If there are any problems, I'll let you know.'

Moira smiled. 'I know you will. You're my best teacher. If every teacher was like you, the world would be a better place.'

'Flatterer,' Lara laughed.

It was nice, though, to be praised. Even if it was by her friend. She and Moira often met up at weekends for a coffee and a chat. Although Moira was about ten years older than her, Lara found her good company, and she had a wicked sense of humour. Moira was a tonic to Lara's tendency to fret.

The head teacher left and Lara calmed her class. The desks were sort of tidied. She decided she'd do a proper job of it once the school bell rang for home. She picked up a book from the library corner and began to read out loud. At once, there was utter silence.

The children leaned in towards her as the story unfolded. She noticed William's face was rapt as she told them about a magic dragon and a boy who had to help defeat the baddies.

The afternoon went along. Lara kept an eye on William. She noticed he didn't speak to anyone. She asked Katie and Ben to play with him at golden hour but he didn't want to. By the end of the school day, she was quite concerned. She didn't want to tell Moira her fears yet. Her pride made her want to sort this out herself.

When the bell went and she released the class, William refused to go. 'Don't you want to go home?' she asked him.

He was sitting in the story corner, flicking through the pages of a colourful picture book. He nodded.

'Then you have to leave the classroom,' Lara said gently. 'Who's coming to collect you today?'

'Dad.'

Well, at least he had a voice, Lara thought. He just didn't want to use it much. She hesitated. 'Why don't I go and get him and bring him here? Then you and Dad can go home together.'

William nodded again. Lara left him amongst the books and went outside to the school gates, where most of the parents and children had gone. She saw Mark out of the corner of her eye, standing at the railings. He started towards her. She ignored him. There was a man right at the gates. He was tall with light brown hair.

'Hello, are you William's Dad?' she called.

He turned relieved eyes to her. 'Yes, where is he?'

'Mr Carter?'

'That's right, I'm Ian Carter.' He glanced at Mark, who'd advanced to within a few feet of them. 'Sorry, am I holding you back from something?'

'Not at all,' Lara said quickly. 'Please come inside with me. William's in the classroom and he won't budge.'

She was glad to get out of Mark's sight. She tried to keep up with Ian

Carter's long stride. He adjusted it almost immediately so that the pace was comfortable.

'Sorry,' he said. 'I'm told I walk too fast. It's very rude of me.'

'Not at all,' Lara said. 'Please don't apologise.' She liked him for saying it, though. He looked anxious, and she knew he must be worried about his son. They got to the classroom and William ran into his father's arms. Ian Carter hugged him tightly, then set him down.

'Now, William, you can't stay at school all night, can you? When Miss . . . ?'

'Miss Perfect. Lara Perfect.'

His lips turned up at her name. She was used to that. It made people smile because it was unusual and funny.

'When Miss Perfect says it's time to leave for home, you have to go outside with the other kids.'

'Okay, Dad,' William whispered, his face turned in to his dad's trousers.

'Why don't you read a little more

while I talk to your dad?' Lara suggested.

She waited until he was back in the corner before speaking again. 'Is there a problem I should know about? William doesn't say much, and he hasn't joined in with the other pupils today.'

'He's very shy,' Ian said.

'Will you be collecting him each day, or will his mum?' Lara asked, trying to build up a picture of William's home life.

'There's just me. My wife died when William was born.'

'I'm so sorry.'

'There's more to it than me being a single dad. The reason we moved here is that William was being bullied in his previous school in the city. There was a group of bigger boys who'd wait for him in the playground after school.'

'So he doesn't want to leave when the bell goes.'

'Exactly.'

Ian Carter's brown eyes met hers square on. Lara realised they weren't really brown at all. They were hazel with flecks of pure green. If she was at all interested in men, which she wasn't, she'd have to say that Ian Carter was a very good-looking guy.

She stared down at her hands in confusion. There was a lot more to life than being good-looking. Mark was handsome too. It was what was inside a person that was important. William's father appeared quite kind and protective of his small son, but she didn't know him at all. And she didn't want to, she reminded herself. He was simply a pupil's parent. It was a professional meeting and she shouldn't be thinking about the colour of his eyes.

'If you want to come into the classroom at the end of day to collect him, that's quite all right,' she said. 'Just until William feels comfortable with his new school. We can work on getting him out of class when the bell goes.'

'Really?' Ian's shoulders relaxed. 'That's great, thank you. I'm working from home, or rather I've set up my office in my uncle's house, so I'm hoping I can get here at three p.m. each day. I'm an architect and can choose my own hours. There might be a problem if I've a client meeting, but I'll try to solve that one.'

'An architect — that sounds very creative,' Lara said. 'I should introduce you to my sister; she's an artist in her spare time.' Then she wondered if she'd been overly familiar. But he smiled at her and she realised she hadn't offended him.

'So you're new to town?' she asked.

'That's right. My uncle isn't well, so we're house-sitting. He's in hospital and he doesn't want to worry about his property lying empty for weeks. It suits us too. Gives me time to look for a house to buy.'

'It's a nice place to bring up kids. There are beautiful woodlands around the town and the sea's not far away, with beaches that are clean.'

At one point Lara had dreamed of bringing up her own kids in the town.

Now that was never going to happen. She had to be content with helping other people's children to thrive.

There was a pause. They both knew the conversation was complete, but it was as if neither wanted the moment to finish. *I'm being fanciful*, Lara thought. *It's just my loneliness coming through. He's probably wishing he was at home with William and away from school and William's new teacher. I'm sure he's got lots of exciting things to do tonight. Unlike me.*

'Can I offer you a lift home?' Ian asked.

'Oh . . . no, I can walk. Thanks anyway,' Lara said.

'You're surprised I asked that,' he said. 'I mean, I don't know you, but you didn't seem very happy to see that chap at the school gate. If he's bothering you, I can drive right past him and he needn't see you.'

Lara felt the tears pricking the backs of her eyes. How kind and thoughtful he was. It would be easy to say yes and avoid Mark. But she couldn't avoid him forever. She shook her head.

'It's very kind of you, but I like to walk. It's the only exercise I get on work days.'

'Very well, I think that's everything. Thanks. Come on William, time to go home.'

She smiled politely as the tall man and the boy went out of the classroom. Maybe she could match make Ian Carter with Kirsty. She knew her sister was looking for a relationship. He was . . . *nice*.

She put on her warm woollen coat and hat, grabbed her bags, and headed out of school. Mark caught her up as she turned the corner onto her own street.

'Wait, Lara. Don't walk so fast.'

She almost slowed when he said that. Then she remembered she didn't need to do what he told her to anymore. So she kept her steps long and fast so that he had to keep up.

'I'm in counselling,' Mark said. 'I've

realised I was the problem, not you. I've got low self-esteem, and that's why I wanted to be better than you. That's why I kept putting you down.'

He was rattling it off as if he'd learnt it by rote. Lara rolled her eyes. There was a part of her that felt sorry for him. There was still a tiny part of her that loved him. But the largest part was screaming 'no'. She didn't have to listen to him. Kirsty would be mad at her for letting him tail along like this. If Kirsty was here, Mark would vanish. He'd never known how to deal with Kirsty's forcefulness. Lara wished she was more like her sister. Kirsty had got all the confidence and sociability genes.

'Lara? See what I'm saying. You can come back to me now. I've changed. At least say you'll meet me for a drink?'

She turned then, as she was almost at the door to her flat. She did not want him demanding to come inside.

'Maybe,' she said, just to get rid of him.

His expression brightened. 'Great. I'll

be in touch.' He walked away with a wave.

Lara groaned. She should have told him no. That there was absolutely no way on earth she was going back to him. But conflict scared her. Instead, she'd managed to imply she might go on a date. She took out her keys with trembling fingers. She needed a coffee and a lie-down. Then she needed a personality transplant.

★   ★   ★

It was later in the evening, and William was in bed. Ian stirred a pot of chilli beef. It was pitch-black outside. He drew down the kitchen blind, and heard the front door open and close. Alan was home.

'Hey, I'm in here,' he called. 'Do you want some chilli?'

'Yes, please. It smells fantastic,' Alan said, coming through on a blast of cold outside air. 'I finally got away from the gallery and managed to sell two paintings. It was worth it, even if I did have to stay late. Uncle Simon will be pleased.'

They cleared a space on the dining room table, sweeping the junk aside.

'You know, we're going to have to clear this place out,' Alan said, taking a mouthful of chilli. 'I don't think Uncle Simon's dusted or tidied in years.'

Ian held up a shirt missing all its buttons. 'I totally agree. This should be in a wardrobe or perhaps the bin, not on the table where we eat. I'm beginning to regret coming north to be with you.'

Alan's spoon froze midway to his mouth. 'You're not really — are you?'

'No.' Ian grinned. 'I'm glad to get a chance to remove William from that appalling school. It'd help to live in a clean, tidy house, though.'

'We'll have a spring clean tomorrow. Or rather, a winter clean. Karen's coming over on Saturday to put up the decorations. You know what a stickler for cleanliness she is.'

The brothers stared at each other; Ian looked away first. He didn't like Karen. He couldn't see what Alan saw in her. But then, he was no guru when it came to understanding women. Since Alicia had died five years ago, he hadn't dated anyone. Lara Perfect's pretty face rose up in his mind spontaneously.

'I met someone today,' he said.

'Yeah?' Alan said, absentmindedly.

Ian reckoned Alan was thinking about Karen and how to totally revamp Uncle Simon's house before the weekend. Karen would blame Alan if the place wasn't perfect.

'She was really . . . *nice*. That doesn't do her justice. But she was. Nice, I mean.' He laughed self-consciously, then stopped abruptly. 'She told me she'd introduce me to her sister as we'd make a good match.'

But I don't want to meet her sister; I like her, Ian thought suddenly. He looked up. Alan was staring at him in fascination.

'You're attracted to this woman. Ian

Carter, my little brother. You finally met a woman you fancy.'

'Firstly, I'm the same height as you, six foot two at the last count. And secondly . . . well, maybe I did.' The words spilled from his mouth.

It was five years since he'd been widowed. Alicia had told him before she died that she wanted him to be happy and to find someone else. He'd told her he never would. And she, in her infinite wisdom, had simply smiled and stroked his cheek. She'd made him promise to try. But Ian had never wanted to. Until now. Lara's sweet expression and beautiful blue eyes drew him like no one else had. He knew he had to see her again.

3

It was trying to snow again. The day had never really brightened beyond a grey gloom, and now it was early evening. Martha wondered why she'd bothered opening the curtains at all. She went round her new bungalow and drew the drapes shut. It took hardly any time, as the house was so small. She couldn't help comparing it to Hambly. In their old home the windows had rattled in winter winds, and the central heating system hadn't quite managed to control the chill draughts. Martha had always held that to be healthier than a modern house with its hermetically sealed rooms. Now here she was with central heating that worked and double-glazed windows. She felt too hot. And bothered.

'I'm a spoilt woman,' she told herself. 'I ought to be happy here.'

She heard Bob whistling upstairs. *He* was happy. Which made it even worse. Because Martha couldn't settle here. It was a neat place. There was a pocket-sized front garden with a tidy lawn bisected by a garden path to the front door. There was a small, manageable back garden of lawn and flower beds. They had a living room, kitchen, bathroom and three bedrooms. All on one ground floor, with no stairs to make them puff and make the bones creak. The ceilings were low, which saved on heating. There was a single garage for the car. The previous owner had installed a garden shed for storage. Really, Martha thought, there was everything she and Bob needed for their old age. The problem was, Martha didn't feel old enough to need this.

'Shall we go travelling?' she'd asked Bob recently. 'While we're still young enough and fit?'

Bob looked at her as if she'd suggested they take a shuttle to Mars. 'Travelling where?' he said. 'There's so much to do here. I want to lay floorboards in the attic, and in the spring I'm planning to buy a greenhouse. It'll have to be a small one, but there's room beside the garden shed. Anyway, what's all this with the young and fit? We're in our sixties, Martha. We're hardly young, and I'm certainly not fit.'

'We're hardly old either,' she'd snapped, then took a deep breath. 'Sorry, I didn't mean to argue with you. It's just . . . it might do us good.'

What she meant was, she was going to scream if this was all she had to look forward to. Their friends Babs and Frank were of a similar age to them, and were currently on a skiing holiday in Italy. Then in the spring they were having a week in Tenerife, and in the summer they were planning a road trip across the States. Martha couldn't ski, so she didn't envy them the sport so much as the chance to experience life and new adventures while they still had the energy to do so. How was she going to lever Bob out of his comfort zone? Was it even possible? She felt her spirits droop.

It was as if he was planning for a decade ahead. She hadn't wanted to leave Hambly, but she hadn't wanted to upset Bob. He was adamant it was for the best. To be fair, he bore the brunt of making repairs to the old house. But they could've paid someone else to do the difficult jobs.

'How about a short cruise?' she said. 'Babs and Frank did that last year and they loved it.'

'I've never seen the point of a cruise. A whole week floating about on the sea.'

'Babs said there was lots to do on board. There were lovely meals and evening entertainment. Besides, you're not on the ship the whole week; there are day trips to interesting places.'

Bob grunted. Martha waited. When he didn't speak, she tried again.

'You've always said you wanted to see the Coliseum in Rome. The thing is, we can. All we have to do is get some brochures and book something. Babs and Frank — '

'Will you stop going on about Babs and Frank? Let's lead our own lives. We don't need to compare ourselves to your friends.'

'They're not *my* friends, they're *our* friends,' Martha said, her voice rising slightly.

'You know what I mean. Stop twisting my words. What is wrong with you these days? You're acting very oddly. Why this sudden desire to travel, for goodness sake? Can't you be happy here?'

'Is it wrong to want more from life than a pair of slippers and a Sunday newspaper?' Martha shouted.

'That's below the belt! I like reading the papers, and those slippers are very comfortable. You gave them to me last Christmas.'

There was an icy silence between them. Martha was fuming. Bob looked hurt. He was good at acting, she thought. He wanted her to apologise. Well, this time she wasn't going to. Instead, she decided not to speak to him. Unfortunately, just at that moment Lara arrived unexpectedly, and obviously sensed an atmosphere. Martha had been forced to sit and eat scones as if nothing was wrong.

Since then, nothing had changed. She sighed and started to lay the table for dinner. The dining area was an open space off the living room. Not like Hambly's big old dining room with its large Victorian dining table. She had been able to sit eight people there. Here, when the four of them got together, there was a squash. No one could quite raise their elbows to eat.

She was looking forward to seeing Kirsty and Lara. It was difficult getting used to them not living in the same house. Even Martha could see that it was good for them to have their independence. As a mother, she was torn between knowing it was a good thing, and missing her girls.

She'd cooked their favourite meal, shepherd's pie, and she was going to serve it up with garden peas and baby carrots. Then for dessert they'd have homemade apple pie with whipped cream. It was comfort food — Martha needed comforting, even if her daughters didn't. She had set the table with her best china, the shepherd's pie was bubbling away in the oven, and the veg were simmering, when the doorbell rang.

'I'll get it,' Bob called. Then she heard him greeting his children fondly. She smiled. It was going to be a nice evening, all four of them together.

'Hello, Mum,' Kirsty said as she breezed into the kitchen. 'Smells great in here.'

Martha turned round to see her, flinging her oven gloves to one side. Kirsty looked lovely. Her dark hair was shiny and pinned up so that tendrils curled over her ears. She was wearing a cream jersey dress with a chunky wooden bead necklace and an embossed leather belt with a turquoise stone buckle.

'Here's a little gift,' Kirsty said, handing over a small package in tissue paper.

Martha unwrapped it carefully to find two tiny wooden reindeer with gold string loops.

'For your Christmas tree. They're from a new range in for the shop, and I thought you'd like these. Aren't they cute?'

'They are indeed. Thank you, darling. Dad and I haven't even thought about getting a tree yet. But when we do, these will be the first decorations on it.'

'No tree? Come on, Mum, it's a week into December already,' Kirsty teased.

Martha smiled at her older daughter. Kirsty adored Christmas and always had. No doubt her flat was already draped in tinsel and all the trimmings. But Martha couldn't summon up any enthusiasm for decorating her new house. It was too painful comparing it to all the Christmases they'd enjoyed at Hambly.

'I'll get around to it soon,' she promised.

'It won't be the same, will it?' Kirsty sighed. 'I'll miss Christmas at Hambly.'

'So will I. But life goes on. We'll have a good one here too.'

'You don't sound too sure. Is everything okay with you and Dad?' Kirsty lifted the oven gloves, folded them and dropped them back on the table, not looking at her.

'Of course it is. Why wouldn't it be?' Martha was determined not to let either of her daughters know the problems she had. Besides, they were just minor issues, she reminded herself. It was all about adjusting.

'I don't know. I got the feeling you didn't want to move when Dad did, that's all.' There was an unspoken question in Kirsty's voice.

'There's nothing to worry about,' Martha said firmly. 'I like your outfit.

You didn't need to dress up for dinner, you know.'

'Oh, I didn't. I'm going out after-wards.'

'Somewhere nice?' Martha tugged the shepherd's pie from the oven and drained the vegetables.

'I've got a date, actually. So I'm going to a pub in the city.'

'Who's the lucky man?'

'I joined an online dating site, and this is my first appointment — if that's what I'm supposed to call it. Although that makes it sound a bit like work, so maybe not.'

'Online dating?' Martha said. 'Oh, Kirsty, is that a good idea? Is it safe? What's the rush to meet someone? Look at me and Dad. We didn't get married until I was thirty-five. You're only twenty-six. There's plenty of time to meet someone the old-fashioned way.'

'I knew you'd say that. Lara won't like it either. But I've thought about it and I've made the decision. It's not like in your day, Mum. You met Dad when he came to work in the same office. I'm in my shop in a small town; I don't work in a team in a busy office in a big city. I'm never going to meet lots of single men if I don't get proactive.'

Martha shook her head. It didn't seem right somehow. She had no idea about online dating, but she'd never known anyone who had done it.

'What if . . . what if the person you meet isn't very nice? What if he's . . . ' She couldn't voice her fears.

'If he's an axe murderer, you mean?' Kirsty laughed. 'It's a lot more likely that I just won't click with him, or vice versa. In which case I'll be honest and say I don't want to meet him again. It'll be fine. And it'll be fun.'

Martha was still shaking her head as they went through to the dining room, carrying trays of food.

'What's the matter?' Lara stood up to hug her mother. 'What's Kirsty done now?'

'She's started online dating,' Martha said.

She exchanged a concerned stare with Lara. Although she loved both her girls equally, Martha had always found Lara easier to deal with. She had a sweet and gentle personality and was loath to argue, whereas Kirsty was stubborn and passionate about all she did. It could be quite exhausting, especially if Martha didn't agree with her about whatever she was doing.

'You didn't,' Lara said to her sister. 'Tell me you're on a wind-up.'

'Why would I wind you and Mum up about that? Honestly, it's no big deal. What do you think, Dad?'

Martha knew that Bob would back Kirsty up, no matter what. Both daughters had their father round their little fingers.

'Just be careful out there,' Bob said, reaching for his cutlery. 'Now let's eat and put any arguments aside. Okay?'

Martha squeezed his shoulder before she sat down. They might have their differences, but they worked well together when it came to parenting.

They'd barely started their meal before Lara returned to the topic. 'Aren't you scared, going to meet a man you don't know? What if he's ugly or got nose hair or he's boring?'

Kirsty grinned. 'I've got my escape plan ready. If it's a disaster, then I'm going to pretend you've texted me and that I need to go.'

'That's a plan,' Lara said, nodding. 'What about safety? What if he's a creep and tries to follow you home?'

Kirsty waved a forkful of peas at her gaily. 'We're meeting in a busy West End pub. I'll get a taxi from the pub door to the train station. No way he can follow. See, I've got it all worked out.'

'I was going to do a bit of match-making myself,' Lara said. 'I've met a guy who'd be perfect for you.'

'How did you manage to meet a single guy when you work alone with a bunch of kids?'

Kirsty sounded quite put out. Martha hid a smile.

'He's one of the parents. He's a single dad, a widower. His son, William, is such a lovely boy, but he's very shy so Ian comes into the classroom to collect him. He's an architect, so he's very creative — that's why I think you and he would be great together. I'm not sure he's going to manage to keep picking William up, because he's got his work and meetings with clients. It's a problem. I might suggest that I keep William for a while after school to work on his shyness and then I could drop him home.'

'Why don't you ask him out?' Kirsty said. 'It sounds like you're quite smitten with him.'

Lara looked horrified. 'No, I'm not. He's a nice guy but I don't think of him like that. I'm simply helping him with his child's school progress.'

Kirsty smirked. 'Really?'

'Yes, really. Besides, after Mark, I've decided I'm never dating again.'

Martha leaned over and touched Lara's arm in sympathy. 'Give it time, love. Mark turned out to be a horror, but there are lots of very nice men out there.'

'That's not what you just told me,' Kirsty said.

'That's different.'

'Mark's been having counselling.' Lara interrupted what looked like the start of one of Kirsty's famous arguments. Or, as she called them, interesting debates.

'Please tell me you're not going back to him,' Martha said.

Bob looked worried too. They had both supported Lara in leaving her fiancé, and had to pick up the pieces of her broken heart too. It hadn't been easy for any of them. Instead of planning a wonderful wedding, Martha had spent hours with her weeping daughter, listening to all her worries.

'Not in a million years,' Lara said. 'But I do feel sorry for him. He's a bit messed up.'

'He messed *you* up,' Kirsty said, heatedly. 'He'd better not pester you, or I'll be round to deal with him.'

'I kind of agreed to meet him for a drink,' Lara said.

'What! Are you completely mad? He's going to try to persuade you to go back to him. You mustn't meet him.' Kirsty jumped up from the table.

Martha stood up too. She began to clear the dirty dishes. Dinner had not been the relaxed affair she'd hoped for. Instead, she was now worrying about both her offspring, on top of her own problems.

Kirsty glanced at her wristwatch. 'I've got to go. Thanks for dinner. And, Lara — promise me you won't see Mark.'

'Okay, I won't. Enjoy your date.'

The sisters kissed each other's cheeks fondly. Then Kirsty dropped a kiss on Bob's head and rushed out of the room. They heard a rustle as she put on her coat and then the slam of the front door. It reverberated through the house. There was a brief silence after it, like a storm had passed through. Which was so often the case when Kirsty was around, Martha thought.

'More dessert, anyone?' she asked.

*   *   *

Kirsty was more nervous than she'd let on. She wasn't going to admit to her mother, or to Lara, how long she'd spent in front of her mirror trying on dresses. The cream jersey was warm on this cold winter's night and fitted well. It matched her new suede knee-length boots too. Then she'd covered the whole ensemble with her thick woollen winter coat and was ready to go. Or was she? Her heart picked up a beat. She'd never done this before. It felt weird, preparing to go on a date with a stranger.

She glanced at her watch again. There was just time to drop off her new painting at Mr Timmons' gallery. She was certain that Alan Carter was there, as she'd seen him inside when she rushed out of her flat to visit her parents. She suspected he was a workaholic like her. In the week he'd been running the gallery, he'd stayed late every single night. She felt sorry for his girlfriend. Here it was, a Friday night, and he was at work.

She had carefully cocooned her painting in bubble wrap and brown paper. It was wedged in the boot of her car, where it couldn't rattle about. She drove up outside her shop and parked. Yes, the gallery lights were blazing cheerfully. She saw a figure inside. Her traitorous heart beat a little faster. Even though she knew Alan Carter was out of bounds and not at all single.

'Stop it,' she whispered. 'He has a girlfriend. And after this evening, I might have a partner too. Alan could become be a friend. That's all.'

4

She pushed open the gallery door with her hip and went in. Alan looked surprised; then he came forward to take the painting.

'Hello, what's this?'

'It's a painting. Your uncle has been kind enough to let me show some of my work in the gallery, and I've sold two.'

Kirsty tried and failed to keep the pride from her voice. She was proud of it. She loved a blank canvas and a set of watercolours or oils and some background music. Then her imagination took off.

Alan took off the wrappings and smiled. 'This is very good. Who is it?'

She came round to his side so they both faced the picture. Kirsty loved doing portraits. People's faces fascinated her as a subject. This particular painting was of an old woman with incongruous large scarlet drop-earrings.

'I have no idea who she is. I was sitting in a park one day up in the city, on a rare day off from the shop, when she came and sat on the bench opposite. I made some sketches of her while I ate my sandwiches. Then I started painting her when I got home that evening. I absolutely loved the fact she had these amazing earrings on.'

'You're very talented,' Alan said. 'I'd be very pleased to hang this in the gallery. I bet it'll sell quickly.'

'Do you think so? That's great. I really appreciate your comments.'

Alan laughed. 'I'm no expert, so I probably shouldn't be saying anything about it. But hey, I like what I see.'

So do I, Kirsty thought, risking a glance at his gorgeous face. She couldn't help herself. She was extremely attracted to him. But it had to stay hidden. 'I thought you must have had experience of running a gallery if Mr Timmons asked you to cover for him.'

Alan was walking back into the

gallery to the large desk at the back. Kirsty followed him.

'No, it was more a matter of desperation for Uncle Simon. He doesn't have anyone else to turn to and he didn't want to shut the gallery. Luckily, I'd just taken an extended leave on my own job when he called for help.'

'What do you usually do for a living?' Kirsty asked.

'I'm a corporate lawyer.'

Alan laid Kirsty's painting gingerly on the desk and was rummaging in the drawers. He came up with a set of ledgers and a bunch of price labels.

'That sounds interesting,' Kirsty said. She peeled the last of the bubble wrap from the corners of the picture frame.

'It really isn't. I can honestly say that running the gallery, even if's only been a little over a week so far, is a lot more fun.'

'That was heartfelt!' Kirsty raised her brows. She wanted to hear more. It was almost as if Alan Carter was running away from something.

He waved her away. 'I won't bore you with the details. Trust me, it's a long and dull story.'

Kirsty opened her mouth to say that actually she'd love to hear it, when her gaze caught the clock face above him on the wall. 'Eeks, I'm going to be late. Can I leave this with you? I'll call in tomorrow and give you whatever info you need.'

'Sure, no worries,' Alan said easily. 'Enjoy your evening.'

He watched as Kirsty ran the length of the small gallery and slammed out of the door. She was a bit of a whirlwind, he thought with amusement. He stared at the portrait. It was very cleverly executed. The play of light and shadow on the old woman's face was wonderful. Alan didn't know much about art, but his instinct told him this was good. Better than good.

He took down one of Uncle Simon's art books from the shelves and flicked it open. He was determined to educate himself. If only corporate law was half as fascinating as this. He'd barely read a page when his mobile phone rang. It was Karen.

'Where are you?'

'I'm at the gallery.'

'At this hour? I can't believe it. I've been waiting for you for an hour. You said you might be up in the city this evening for a drink.'

'With the emphasis on 'might'. And I said that a couple of days ago when you rang. I hadn't made any firm plans for tonight. Look, I'm really sorry, but there's so much to do here. In fact . . . why don't you drive down and meet me here? It'll only take you a half hour. You can help me tidy up a bit, and then we'll have a drink in the pub down the road.'

'I'm amazed they even have a pub in a tiny place like that. Or is it full of farmers and dockers? I'm not driving down there, Alan. It's Friday night and the West End is beckoning. You need to drive to me and we'll go out.'

Alan knew he was in the wrong. He'd neglected Karen all week in favour of Uncle Simon's delightful gallery. But the previous weekend had been a disaster, and he knew he was avoiding her. He had the impression she'd come looking for a fight. It had started over the state of Uncle Simon's house and the Christmas decorations, but deep down it was about something very different.

Karen had barely got inside the house when she'd screwed her face up in disgust. 'What a midden. I can't believe you're both living in such a dump.'

And this was after Alan and Ian had spent two days clearing up. 'Hello to you too,' Ian said cheerfully.

'Hello, Auntie Karen,' William said, and then hid behind a large picture book he was reading.

'You don't expect me to stay here, Alan, do you?' Karen said, ignoring their greetings.

'It's not that bad. You should've seen

it a few days ago. I know it's a bit untidy, but at least the place is a lot cleaner than it was. Once you've got your bags in and had a cup of tea, you'll feel better.'

'Tea? I don't think so. Pour me a large gin and tonic. Did you get the Christmas decorations I told you to buy?'

'Yes, I did. Here they are. There's no hurry to put them up, is there? Let's relax first and chat with Ian and William.'

Karen was already peeling the seals from the packages and frowning at the baubles.

'This isn't the right shade of blue. I told you marine-blue. This is eggshell-blue.'

'Is it? Sorry. It looked all right to me. The shop owner was very helpful. Look, she got me matching napkins and crackers.'

A grimace caused a sharp line to appear around Karen's coral lips. Alan sighed inwardly. Did it matter what shade of blue the glass balls were? He was pretty sure the answer to that, in the greater scale of life, was no. Why did Karen pick on tiny details? She was never satisfied. Then he felt guilty about his negative thoughts. He tried to look more interested as she complained about the quality and the fact he hadn't bought enough of the decorations to do the whole room and the tree.

He noticed Ian and William slink out of the sitting room and wished he could follow them. Another disloyal thought. The trouble was, he was no longer certain how he felt about Karen. They had been together for two years, and she'd hinted recently she wanted to get engaged. It had made him focus more on their relationship. Did he want to marry her?

They'd met when she joined the law firm Alan worked for. He'd been smitten immediately by her beauty. She had long honey-blonde hair and green eyes, and she dressed to impress. He'd asked her out the day she started and she'd accepted. All was well while Alan worked as a corporate lawyer. But for various reasons, he'd needed a break. Karen hadn't taken well to that. Now here he was living in a small town, while she still lived in the city. Something had to give. He just wasn't sure what that was going to be.

She hadn't relaxed all weekend. She nagged until Alan and Ian scrubbed the floors and walls in the rooms they'd already cleaned. Apparently they weren't clean enough. She spent the time putting up the blue and white decorations. She'd brought along an artificial tree, which was then hung with precision with crystal white lights to match the blue and white theme.

'An artificial tree is so much better than a real one. It won't shed any needles — and look, the branches are perfectly even. This design is the same as that in the magazine I read. It's what all the celebs are after this year.'

In the evening, William wanted them all to play his favourite board game, but

Karen declared herself exhausted and watched sulkily with a glass of wine while the three of them sat with the dice and counters. A slow annoyance was building in Alan. She made no effort to join in or accommodate them. It was all about her. Which was when he began to realise they had no future together.

Actually, it wasn't as sudden as that, he acknowledged. This had been coming for a while. They had different aims for the future. Perhaps he hadn't voiced his loudly. Maybe it was his fault Karen seemed perpetually discontented. She was very ambitious. She wanted a promotion at work and had been very angry when she lost out to another colleague for a recent vacancy. Alan had overheard the senior partners discussing the appointment. The candidate who'd got the job worked well in a team. Karen, they agreed, did not.

'Alan?' Karen's voice down the phone brought him back to the present.

'Yes, still here.'

'I said you need to drive over to me and we'll go out. There's a great new place opened up that I can take us to. One or two well-known actors have been seen there.'

'Thanks, but I think I'll give it a miss tonight. As I said, I've a bit to do here before I shut up shop for the night. I'll give you a call tomorrow, okay?'

She cut him off as he finished speaking. Alan stared at the mobile's screen for a moment and then put the phone down carefully. He sat there for a long while, not moving. To anyone looking in, it was as if he was asleep sitting up. Alan's mind was busy. There were decisions to be made.

★ ★ ★

Kirsty smoothed her jersey dress with damp palms. She had bought a lemonade and was sitting at a table where she could see who came into the bar. She tried to look relaxed, as if she came out to the pub on her own often. In fact, she'd never done so. She met friends usually. She'd deliberately chosen a city pub where she knew nobody. She had her mobile ready in her handbag if she needed to call Lara. Her throat was dry. She took another sip of her drink and coughed on the bubbles.

'Hello, are you Kirsty?'

She glanced up to see a thin young man with a pronounced Adam's apple. It was bobbing about, and his handshake was clammy as he sat down.

'I'm Adrian. Oh, would you like another drink?' He leapt up again.

'No, I'm fine with this one, thanks.'

'I'll get myself a drink then and be back very quickly.'

Kirsty found herself relaxing. Adrian, her date for tonight, was clearly a lot more nervous than her. Strangely, that helped. He managed to spill his drink over the table as he sat down. They both leapt up.

'Sorry, so sorry.'

'It's okay, I'll get a dishcloth from the

barmaid.' Kirsty went over to the bar.

The barmaid came and wiped the table and kindly refilled Adrian's drink. Then there was an awkward silence. Kirsty desperately searched for something intelligent to say. Adrian's Adam's apple went into overdrive.

'Do you like golf?' he said suddenly.

'I've never played it.'

'Oh.'

Silence again.

'I thought we could play a game . . . together . . . next weekend.'

'I don't really like sport.'

'I don't only play golf. I'm a model railway enthusiast.'

'Can I get you another drink?' Kirsty asked.

Without waiting for an answer, she rushed from the table to the bar. What a disaster. They had nothing in common and she didn't fancy him one little bit. She looked at her watch. The minutes were crawling past. She bought two glasses of white wine and took them back. Somehow she was going to have to extricate herself without hurting his feelings.

He looked up eagerly as she came back. He took a great gulp of the wine and a flush rose up on his face.

'I really like you, Kirsty. I'm so glad we're dating. If you don't want to play golf next Saturday, how about I show you my model railway I built? It's in my garage, and it's an authentic replica of the main railway line in Liverpool.'

'Oh, that's my mobile ringing. Will you excuse me, please, Adrian? I need to take the call. It's probably my sister. She's . . . well, she's . . . got a few problems. I might have to leave.'

★   ★   ★

Kirsty managed to get a train home without a long wait. She arrived back on her street feeling she'd hardly been out. Poor Adrian. He'd been very nice when she said she had to go. He'd shouted after her that he'd call. Kirsty pretended not to hear that. She'd have to email him and tell him that she wouldn't be seeing him again. This dating lark wasn't easy.

She hesitated on the doorstep in front of her shop. There were still lights on in the gallery, although she couldn't see Alan. She stared up at the dark windows of her flat above her shop. They were blank and unwelcoming. She didn't want to go home immediately. She wanted some company. On impulse she tried the gallery door. It opened and she went inside.

'Alan?' she called.

He appeared from another room at the back. 'Are you all right?' he said.

'Yes, I . . . I'm bothering you. I should go.' She turned on her heels to flee. It had been a bad idea.

'No, wait! Have a seat. I could do with a break.' He grinned and indicated the plastic chairs where they'd sat earlier to admire her painting.

'Thanks. I've had an awful evening.'

'What a shame. You looked dressed

for a party. Am I allowed to ask what went wrong?'

'I had a date,' Kirsty said, and shook her head. 'It was terrible. I didn't know what to say to him and it turned out we liked completely different things. I'm not sure if I can handle meeting the next guy.'

'The next guy?' Alan sounded puzzled.

Kirsty laughed. 'That sounds awful, doesn't it? I've joined an online dating site, you see, and tonight was my first date. He was a nice enough chap, but not for me. I've got another one lined up for tomorrow night.'

Alan frowned. 'Is it safe meeting strangers like that?'

Kirsty had been angry with her mother and sister for voicing the same concerns. But when Alan did so, she was oddly pleased that he was concerned for her.

'You sound like my mum,' she teased. 'Seriously, it's fine. There's plenty of common-sense advice on how to meet up and stay safe.'

Alan grinned. 'I won't ask any more. I don't want to be accused of being your mother.'

Kirsty smiled back.

'Would you like a cup of tea?' Alan asked. 'I was about to put the kettle on.'

'That would be lovely. Can I help?'

But Alan said he'd manage. Kirsty waited in the gallery and looked at the paintings. Mr Timmons had a good eye for art. Some of the pieces were stunning. With no false pride, Kirsty was confident her painting would sit well with the others. She hoped it'd sell. Back at the desk, she noticed an art book open on it. She flicked through it, and then Alan arrived with two mugs of steaming tea.

'I'm trying to educate myself.' He nodded at the book in Kirsty's hands.

'Would you like to have your own gallery?'

'I've dreamed about it. It's a far step from being a lawyer. Maybe a step too far.'

'Is that why you took a career break?'

'I don't know. I only know that I can't be a corporate lawyer for the rest of my life. I'd love to do something creative. Running this gallery is giving me a taste of what that'd be like. Having this time away from my job was meant to give me space, so I can work out what on earth I'm going to do with the next few years.'

'Wow,' Kirsty breathed. 'That's hard.'

'Harder than I thought it'd be. If I follow my heart, then I'm going to have to give up the large wage packets and learn to live more simply.'

Kirsty wondered what Alan's girlfriend thought about his plans. She'd started off going out with a wealthy lawyer, but then all of a sudden she wasn't. That could test the strongest of relationships. She didn't know Alan well enough to ask about that. The expression on his face suggested some turmoil.

'My mum and dad always advised Lara and me to do what we enjoyed.'

'They sound like great parents. Your sister, Lara — I don't suppose she's a school teacher, is she?'

'She is! Why? Have you met her?'

'No, but my brother, Ian, has. She's been very helpful settling my nephew into his new school.'

'Your brother is Ian? Lara's mentioned him. It's a small world.'

Alan grinned. 'It is in this town. It's very different from living in the city. I like it.'

'Me too.'

Kirsty did like living in the town where she'd grown up. But it had got a whole lot more interesting since Alan and his brother Ian had come to live there.

5

Lara's head was thumping, and it wasn't just because primary one had been practising their singing for the school show all afternoon. She blew her nose again and crumpled the paper hanky with a heartfelt sigh. A quick glance in her compact mirror showed reddened eyes and a nose that Rudolf would have been proud to own.

'Are we going now, miss?' William asked.

They were both in Lara's classroom. The school day was finished, and William had been reading quietly while Lara tidied up. Lara had spoken to Ian Carter and suggested that she take William home with her each school day until Ian could pick him up. He'd been very grateful. The problem was that his client meetings meant that his original plan to be at the school gates for three o'clock hadn't worked out. Lara was happy to have William's company. She was becoming very fond of him. She was pleased, too, that William was beginning to speak in class and now played with Ben and Katie at break time.

'Yes, let's go,' she croaked. Her throat was raw and scratchy. She hoped she didn't pass her cold on to William.

'Your voice sounds funny.'

'I'm not feeling too good,' she said. 'Never mind. I'll make us some hot chocolate; that'll help.'

'Will I get some, even if I'm not ill?'

Lara laughed but it turned into a coughing fit. She nodded her head and grabbed her pack of hankies. 'Of course you will. I might even have a biscuit to go with it.'

'Can we go and get it now?'

'Let's do that,' Lara agreed, slinging her handbag over her shoulder and picking up a large pile of jotters. She had marking to do that evening. Her head was so woolly, she wondered if she'd manage it.

They left the school and walked across the playground. William halted suddenly and his hand slid into hers.

'What is it?'

'That man's waiting for you again.'

Lara glanced up to see Mark at the gates. She groaned inwardly. She really didn't need this today. Not when she was feeling so awful. She remembered her promise to Kirsty and hoped Mark wasn't going to press for them to go to the pub.

'Don't worry, William. He's . . . an old friend of mine, that's all.' Her voice didn't sound convincing, even to her.

William threw her a worried look. She forced a smile. She pulled the child with her and they went on through the gates onto the pavement.

'There you are, Lara,' Mark said, looking cross. 'Why are you so late out of work? I've been waiting ages.'

Nobody asked you to, Lara thought, but she didn't say it out loud. She didn't want to start an argument with him. Right now, she wanted simply to run away and hide under her pillow. Her headache was worse. It was as if there was a steel band around her temples. She gripped William's hand in hers and hugged the pile of jotters with her other arm.

'You haven't changed a bit, have you, Lara? You always were so vague when I asked you a direct question,' he continued.

She didn't like his angry tone. But she was somehow conditioned not to answer back. Instead, she shied away. Mark took a step towards them. Lara thought that his therapy hadn't helped him much. This was like the old Mark. The Mark that bullied her relentlessly. The Mark that inevitably got what he wanted. Usually at Lara's expense.

A tall figure loomed into view. 'Is this guy bothering you, Lara?'

Relief at hearing Ian Carter's deep voice flooded through her. William ran to his dad. Lara grabbed at the slipping jotters but it was too late; they scattered to the ground. Mark kicked at them as they landed on his shoes. In dismay, Lara saw the muddy foot marks on the covers. Focussed on the damage to her class's hard work, she didn't notice Ian moving in front of Mark. Nor did she see both men's muscles flex and tense, ready for a fight. Ian's expression was grim, and Mark quickly guessed who'd win any outright contest. By the time she looked up, her ex-fiancé had gone.

Ian crouched beside her and helped gather up the jotters. 'I'm giving you a lift home today and I'm not taking no for an answer,' he said.

Lara's hands were shaking. She tried to hide it by holding onto the jotters. 'I'd be very grateful if you could drop me off,' she said.

They didn't speak much on the short journey to Lara's flat. She sneezed and blew her nose and mumbled her apologies. Ian concentrated on driving, with a few concerned glances in Lara's direction. William sat nicely in his car booster seat and stared at both of them with interest.

'Here we are,' Ian said, coming round to the passenger side to open the door for Lara.

'Thanks for the lift,' Lara said, then coughed. She felt rotten. For a fleeting moment she felt sorry for herself. There was no one waiting at home to make her hot chocolate to soothe her throat. There was no one to comfort her. There never had been. Mark wasn't that sort. Maybe she should go home to her parents. Her mother would look after her.

'You look rough,' Ian said, taking the jotters from her. 'We'll come up with you and make sure you're all right.'

'There's no need.'

'Perhaps not, but I'd like to anyway. It'll put my mind at ease if I know you're okay.'

'It's only a cold. But it's very nice of you to bother.'

'No bother at all,' Ian said firmly, following her and William up the neat flat stairwell to Lara's top-floor flat.

She fumbled with her house keys before managing to unlock the door. By now, her head was thick with the cold. She was glad she kept her flat tidy. She didn't want Ian to think she was someone who lived in a mess — even if it was true sometimes.

'Miss Perfect is going to make hot chocolate,' William piped up hopefully. 'And she's got biscuits.'

'Remember, you can call me Lara when we're outside school,' Lara murmured, sinking back into the couch.

'I don't think Lara is in a fit state to make anyone hot chocolate,' Ian told William.

His son looked downcast. 'Can't you make it, Dad? I don't think it's hard to do.'

Ian looked queryingly at Lara. She nodded. 'If you don't mind doing it, the kitchen's through that door there.'

'I don't mind at all. William, do you want to help me?'

'I can put the biscuits on a plate,' William said.

Ian and Lara smiled at each other over the top of his head.

Lara settled against the couch, feeling marginally better just for being at home. It was nice, she thought, having Ian and William here. The flat could sometimes be a little lonely.

She often put the radio on for company to block out the silence. She missed her room at Hambly. Still, it was important to grow up and move on. She wouldn't have wanted to live at Hambly forever. It was just a shame that she couldn't go there to visit her parents. The new house didn't have the same draw. She hoped her mum and dad would grow to like it.

In the kitchen, there were the sounds of chatter and the clink of ceramics. Then she heard the kettle going on. They were simple everyday noises, so why did they make her feel so happy? Ian was a lovely man, she decided. She couldn't imagine Mark, in a million years, making her hot chocolate when she was ill. Any time she'd been poorly, he'd always had it worse. She ended up looking after him. Or he complained she was neglecting him if she cancelled a night out. Worse, she'd been forced to go out with his friends when she was ill because Mark didn't tolerate being told no.

William was back. He sat on the carpet next the couch and stared at her.

'What is it?' she asked. 'Did you find the biscuit packet?'

William nodded. 'Dad's got it.'

There was a pause, then he said, 'That man was bullying you.'

Lara considered this. 'Yes, he was.'

'You said he was your friend.' William sounded indignant.

'I thought he was my friend . . . a very good friend. But it turns out I was wrong.'

'I didn't know adults got bullied.'

'I suspect that children who are bullies grow up into adults who bully,' Lara said sadly.

William stroked the carpet. He kept his eyes on it. 'I was bullied, at my other school. They said they were my friends too. But they weren't.'

'What did you do?'

'Dad said I wasn't to show them I was scared. So I tried. But it didn't work. I can run fast, so I did that.'

Lara smiled wryly. She should do that. Show Mark she wasn't scared of him. Even if she was inside. It was hard though. 'I can't run fast at all,' she said.

'Oh dear,' William said. Then he brightened. 'I know, Dad can tell that man to go away. My Dad's very brave.'

I wish I was, Lara thought.

Ian came through with a tray of hot drinks and a plate of biscuits. 'How do you feel?' He leant over and placed one large hand on Lara's brow.

If she'd felt hot before, she fairly sizzled now.

'You've got a temperature. Once we've had our hot chocolate and left you in peace, you ought to go to bed. It might be flu. I can get your groceries, if you tell me what you need.'

'You don't have to do that,' Lara protested feebly.

Ian laughed. 'I don't have to, no. But I want to. I'm not leaving you here to starve away on your own. Actually, do you have anyone you want me to call to say you're ill?'

Lara stared at him. He was so kind. She hardly knew him and yet he was doing all this for her. 'Thanks, but I can do that. My sister Kirsty can do the shopping for me too.'

'Ahh, the famous Kirsty,' Ian teased her gently. 'I believe my brother Alan has met her.'

'That's right; Kirsty told me about you and Alan being brothers and how Alan's running the gallery next to her shop.' The hot chocolate was soothing on Lara's throat, and she perked up a little.

William munched on biscuits. He hummed tunes to himself. It was better than the radio, Lara decided.

'Alan's certainly enjoying his new

occupation,' Ian said.

'What about you? Are you enjoying your job here?'

'I love being an architect, and the job travels well. That's why it's been so easy moving here. The internet and email make the world smaller.'

'Kirsty has an online shop,' Lara said, thinking again how suited her sister and Ian would be. 'She actually sells more online than she does in her real shop.'

'It's the way things are going, isn't it? It's a pity, really. I like seeing real shops, especially bookshops,' Ian said, finishing the last of his drink and putting the mug down on the tray.

'I totally agree,' Lara said, nodding. 'I love browsing bookshops, but there are so few these days.'

'I noticed there is an independent bookshop in the next town, on the seafront. Perhaps we could go there for a browse sometime?'

Lara flushed. How awful of her. Poor Ian must've thought she was hinting at a date with him. She hadn't meant that at all. It was just nice to find someone who thought the same way.

'I don't know . . . I'm quite busy with . . . with work, and of course Christmas coming up.' She wanted to kick herself for her awkwardness. She hoped he'd put her high colour down to her flu.

'Of course,' he said easily. 'Anyway, William and I must get going. Look after yourself and go straight to bed.'

When they'd gone, Lara took the tray through to her kitchen. She'd been going to wash and dry the mugs but suddenly she had no energy. She left them on the tray with their dregs of hot chocolate and a few crumbs of biscuits on the plate. Then she stumbled into her bedroom, lay on the bed and fell fast asleep.

* * *

Ian could have kicked himself. What an idiot he was! He'd totally messed up asking Lara out. He had to put it down to lack of practice. The last time he'd asked a woman out, it was Alice, and that had been ten years ago. Anyway, judging by Lara's reaction, she didn't want to go out with him. There was something going on between her and the man who was at the school gates. He wanted to ask Lara about that but he didn't know her well enough to pry.

'Dad . . . ' William tugged at his hand.

'What is it, son?'

'You have to help Miss Perfect, I mean Lara. She doesn't like that man. He's bullying her.'

All Ian's protective instincts rose up. He was shocked to find that he would've quite happily punched the guy on the nose if he hadn't backed off. When had he become so primitive? When he'd seen saw Lara's distress, he'd known. He couldn't bear the thought of her being unhappy or scared.

'Daaaad.'

'I hear you,' Ian said. 'I'm thinking how I can help her.'

'That's good, because I like her.'

'Me too.'

'Can we have pizza for tea?'

Ian let the conversation turn to food. They argued over the healthiness of pizza, and whether William needed to eat two kinds of vegetables with his dinner or only one. They went home via the supermarket, where Ian ended up buying three frozen pizzas. He also got a selection of fresh veg to balance the guilt. William sneaked a tub of ice cream into the trolley and Ian pretended not to notice until he'd paid for it all. They took the carrier bags of groceries out to the car, William skipping beside him.

Then William stopped. 'You never got any food for Lara.'

'She said her sister would get it.'

'No, you were to get it,' William insisted.

Ian tried to remember back to the conversation. There was a large part of him that would love to call in on Lara again so soon. He loved seeing her pretty face and sweet smile. He loved being with her. There was another part of him that felt embarrassed at asking her out. If he went back to her flat, she might think he was pushing his attentions on her. A bit like that other guy.

'I'm pretty sure that Kirsty is going to be bringing Lara her groceries,' Ian said firmly. The small cowardly part of him had won out. William seemed to accept what he said, and so they went home. Well, Ian thought, it wasn't home, it was lodgings. Although Uncle Simon had a large house, it wasn't theirs. He needed to find a place soon for himself and William.

The house was empty. He guessed Alan was at the gallery. His brother spent most hours there, very absorbed in his tasks. The landline red light flashed. Ian pressed for messages. Four from Karen. Alan was to call her when he got them. They had to talk. She wasn't going to let him ruin everything. Not when she'd worked so hard for them both. He was being ridiculously selfish.

'What's Auntie Karen saying?' William asked.

'I don't know,' Ian said, although he could take a guess at what Alan had done.

'Will Uncle Alan want his pizza?'

'He will want it later when he comes home. Come on, let's get the table set for dinner. You can lay the cutlery and glasses.'

As Ian prepared their dinner, he hoped Alan had broken it off with Karen. Her behaviour when she'd visited had been appalling. He'd avoided her as much as possible. Then he'd felt bad leaving Alan to bear the brunt of her bad mood. The decorations, in their cold blue and white colours, were a reminder of that endless weekend. He hated artificial trees. He liked the smell of pine needles. He even liked the way they dropped everywhere. It was part of the charm and fun of the festive season. Out of loyalty to Alan, he hadn't voiced this. He didn't care that much about the decorations.

After dinner, he played board games with William. Then they watched television until the cartoon channel went to bed. At this point, it was time for William's bed too. The little boy was yawning as he protested he didn't need to sleep.

'I'll read you a story if you get ready double quick,' Ian promised.

When William was tucked up in bed, Ian went through. He picked a favourite book and sat down on the end of the bed.

'Did Mummy have blue eyes?' William said.

Ian was startled. He carefully put the book down on the duvet. William didn't ask about Alice much. He had never known her. Only occasionally did he ask about her.

'Mummy had brown eyes and dark brown hair. She was very beautiful and she loved you very, very much. You know she had brown eyes. I've shown you pictures of her.'

William yawned and rubbed his face. 'Lara has blue eyes. They look like the sky. Do you think Lara's beautiful?'

'She's very pretty,' Ian said. 'But you know it doesn't matter what someone looks like on the outside; it's what's inside that matters.'

'I think she's very pretty on the inside too,' William mumbled as his head touched the pillow and his eyes shut tight.

Ian leaned over and kissed his son's soft cheek.

6

Kirsty's Christmas shop was busy. She'd poured cinnamon and clove essences onto an oil lamp, and the sweet aromas wafted around the crowded space. Two couples and a family were browsing, and Kirsty was engrossed in wrapping a toy tractor for a pleased grandmother. Outside, it was a deep velvety black despite the afternoon hour.

'My grandson will love that tractor,' the woman said with a smile. 'I've nearly finished my Christmas shopping. Have you done yours?'

'You'd think that me owning a Christmas shop, I'd be all prepared weeks in advance,' Kirsty laughed. 'But the truth is, I haven't even begun.'

'Not long to go — the days are flying past,' her customer said. 'Thank you for wrapping this so nicely. You've got a real knack for it.'

One satisfied customer, thought Kirsty, smiling to herself as the woman went out, making the bell chime merrily. She helped the family choose presents for their cousins, who were coming up to stay for the holidays. She got all the details from the excited children while their mother fondly rolled her eyes above their heads at her. The two couples chose items carefully amidst much discussion. Her last customer had just left, and Kirsty was considering filling the teapot once again, when the lights suddenly went out.

She was left fumbling in the dark. The street lights outside the windows helped, plus there was the tiny candle under the oil lamp. Kirsty checked her till. It was out too. There must have been a power cut or something. She had no idea about electricity. For a moment she stood there, undecided.

Then she carefully found her way into the back room and got her coat. Pulling it on snugly, she hurried next door. The gallery's lights were blazing cheerfully. Clearly, whatever the problem was, it was confined to her shop. Frowning, she went in.

'Hey there,' Alan called, coming toward her with a grin.

She found herself grinning back. Then she remembered why she was there.

'Something the matter?' Alan asked as her smile dropped away and her dark brows knitted in consternation.

'My whole shop's been plunged into darkness.'

'Has a fuse gone?'

'I haven't a clue.'

'Shall I come and have a look at it?'

'That would be great,' Kirsty said. 'I know I ought to be able to fix stuff myself, but I admit I'm not very good with DIY. Now if my dad was here, he'd know what was wrong. He's a marvel with fixing things.'

'No pressure on me then,' Alan joked.

'Oh, I didn't mean . . . '

'I'm teasing. Now come on, let's go and get the lights back on.'

Kirsty led the way. There was a toolbox in the back room, which she gave to Alan. She sat at her desk while he tinkered with the fuse box and went into the shop front. He soon had the lights back on.

'That's a miracle,' Kirsty said. 'Thanks.'

'Less of a miracle, more a case of the lights being tripped. I've replaced the fuse in one of the plugs and all is well.'

They stood looking at each other. Alan handed back the toolbox. Kirsty stacked it in a corner. He scratched his head. She jingled her keys. Then they both spoke at once.

'Fancy a cup of coffee?'

'Will you stay for a cuppa?'

Alan grinned. Kirsty thought how much she liked it when he did. It made him even more gorgeous, if that was possible.

'Your place or mine?' she joked, and then winced. It sounded like the worst kind of pick-up line. 'I meant . . . '

'I know what you meant. Look, I offered you coffee, so why don't we go back to the gallery and I'll brew some up? Unless you're staying open, that is.'

Kirsty shook her head. 'It's almost five now. I'm shutting up shop for today. I'd be very glad of a hot cup of coffee.'

She took her bag and locked up and they both went next door. It was warm and cosy in the gallery, with soft music playing in the background and the scent of lemon wood polish. Kirsty admired the paintings again. Alan made coffee and brought it out.

'So your dad's a bit of a handyman, is he?'

'Yes, he can fix anything,' Kirsty said, sipping her coffee. 'When he and Mum lived at Hambly, Dad was forever up on the roof fixing loose tiles. There were plenty of those.'

'Hambly?'

'It was our family home.' She told him about growing up in Hambly and how it had recently been sold.

'You miss it.' It was a statement, not a question.

'I do, I really do. Their new house is soulless. That sounds terrible, but that's how it feels. Whereas Hambly was full of character and quirkiness.'

'How do your parents feel?' Alan asked. He looked very relaxed, leaning back in his chair with one leg crossed over his other knee. Kirsty felt relaxed in his company too. It was nice to have someone to talk to. She could always talk to Lara, of course; but that was different, being family.

'I don't know exactly. I think Dad's quite happy about the move, but Mum's a bit cagey.'

'Give it time,' Alan said. 'It's amazing how something that seems insurmountable is suddenly resolved a few months down the line.'

'Are you speaking from experience? That sounded quite heartfelt.'

Alan sighed and put his coffee cup down. 'I think I'm still at the stage where it's insurmountable, but the advice is sound. I got it from my brother. Ian's been through a lot; his wife passed away.'

'I'm sorry to hear that.'

'It was five years ago, but I guess it never heals entirely. I admire Ian for the way he's kept it together for William.'

'What about you? What's blocking you?' Kirsty asked.

'I'm blocking myself. Yes, I believe that's what it is. I told you I'm a corporate lawyer, but my heart isn't in it. Hasn't been for a long while. But somehow it's harder to extricate yourself from a life path than you might think.'

'So you'd like to run a gallery?'

'Yeah, but . . . it's a risk.'

'Life's a risk,' Kirsty said, 'but you've got to follow your passions. Otherwise, what's the point? Look at me. Mum and Dad were very worried when I said I wanted to run a Christmas shop. They wanted me to go to university and study for something sensible, like nursing or teaching. But I always knew what I wanted to do. And yes, it was a risky business investing in a shop, but it's been worth it. I'm so happy doing what I'm doing. Isn't that what it's all about?'

'You make it sound so simple.'

'It doesn't have to be complicated. All you need is determination and a huge amount of energy,' Kirsty laughed.

'That sort of sounds simple. Did you notice the sign on the coffee shop next door?'

The gallery was flanked by Kirsty's Christmas shop on one side and a cheerful mid-range coffee shop on the other. Kirsty shook her head. 'Can't say I've noticed anything. Mind you, I've been rushed off my feet lately with all the Christmas shoppers. What's the deal?'

Alan's eyes lit up and Kirsty saw his excitement. 'There's a for-sale sign on it.'

'Wow, I didn't know Lisa was selling up. She's been there for about fifteen years. I guess she's at retirement age. She was telling me about some exotic holidays she and her husband have lined up. She never mentioned the coffee shop, though.'

'Maybe she only just decided. Anyway, I've had this idea. I don't know if Uncle Simon will go for it.'

'For what?'

'It would be possible to knock through the wall between the gallery and the coffee shop. Imagine, we'd have more space to show the art, and people could browse and sit and have a cappuccino too.'

'Oh, that sounds wonderful,' Kirsty said, catching his infectious enthusiasm. She could almost see the place as Alan proceeded to describe his vision for the gallery extension. His voice trailed off a little uncertainly.

'What is it?' Kirsty urged. 'It's a great idea. Simon would have to be mad not to go for it.'

'I don't know. He's quite conservative; likes things to stay the same.

Perhaps I'm overstepping the mark with this.'

'No, you're not. You've got to discuss it with him. When he's better, of course. That gives you a few weeks to really sketch this out, get some quotes, ask Lisa what she wants for the coffee shop and so on.'

'You think so?'

'Honestly, I do. I think it'd be great for Simon's business and great for the town.'

Alan stared at her for a moment, as if he was trying decide something. Just as his piercing gaze began to make Kirsty shuffle, he spoke. 'Can I show you something?'

'Sure.'

'It's at home. I know you live upstairs, but I'll drop you back.'

'Okay, I'm intrigued now.'

It was only a short drive to Simon's house. There was a welcoming glow of lights from the windows as they parked in front of it. 'My brother Ian and his son will be in,' Alan warned. 'It might be quite messy; William likes to help with the cooking.'

'It's a great skill to have,' Kirsty said, thinking of her own flat where her fridge was home to a piece of cheese and a half bottle of milk. She often ate takeaways or went home to Martha for a decent meal. Cooking was not one of her strengths.

They were met by the aroma of tomato sauce and garlic. 'Smells delicious,' Kirsty murmured.

'Stay for dinner,' Ian said as he came towards them, hand outstretched to meet Kirsty. 'William made the pasta sauce and he's very proud of it.' He winked and whispered, 'He did the stirring, in any case.'

A small boy appeared, wearing a tomato-stained chef's apron and wielding a dripping wooden spoon. 'Are you Miss Perfect's sister?'

'Yes, I'm Kirsty. I forgot that Lara's your teacher. Is it okay if I stay to eat your tomato pasta dish?'

William nodded fervently. 'Dad says

it needs more pepper. Do you want to see if he's right?'

Kirsty found herself following him into the kitchen. Alan had been right; it was a mess. There was an explosion of flour, chopped-tomato cans and onion peelings. Underfoot, there was pasta crunching where it had been spilt. There were sticky red handprints on the surfaces. But the meal bubbled in a large pan, and nearby, the kitchen table was neatly set for dinner. Ian came in and swiftly laid another place for Kirsty.

'Do you mind me staying?' she asked, feeling she was intruding.

'Not at all,' he said easily. 'It's nice to have company. How's Lara?'

'She's feeling pretty awful. I'm going over tonight to take her some supplies. I'll tell her you asked after her.'

Was that a faint blush on Ian's cheeks? Kirsty hid a smile. Lara might deny her interest in Ian, but it looked as if he was interested in her little sister, without a doubt.

Dinner was a relaxed affair. There

were bowls of pasta, plates of crusty homemade garlic bread and a green salad. The three adults chatted on a variety of topics, with William chipping in too. Kirsty liked that Ian and Alan both listened to the child and answered him seriously on his many questions. She decided that Lara could do a lot worse than go out with Ian, if she gave up on her ridiculous decision never to date again. She had to get over Mark. Let the past go. She was too young to give up on having a happy future.

'So, can I show you what I invited you over to see?' Alan said after they'd washed down a slice of cake with a small strong coffee.

'Yes, please. I'm curious to know what it is.'

Alan motioned her to go with him. Ian waved her away as she hesitated over the dirty dishes on the table. 'Go on,' he said, 'I'll manage this. It's Alan's turn to clear up tomorrow.'

She smiled, liking him even more, and went after Alan up the stairs. On the way, she glanced over at the living-room decorations. Someone had gone to a lot of bother putting up an artificial tree and arranging the baubles and tinsel methodically. She pulled a wry expression. The decorations were from her shop and they had proved very popular, but she still couldn't bring herself to like them. They were too cold somehow. Too precise. But, she thought, it was good that different people liked different styles, otherwise life would be dull. It was just slightly . . . disappointing that Alan's taste was so different from her own. After all, even though his girlfriend had sent him to buy them, he hadn't said that he didn't like them.

Upstairs, he opened a box room at the end of the corridor. 'This is Uncle Simon's storeroom, but I've cleared a space. What do you think?'

The room was stacked high with books and journals and odds and ends. In the middle of the floor there was an easel. Attached to it was a small unframed picture. Kirsty leaned in for a good look. It was a neat watercolour of a house in a sandy bay. What lifted it out of the ordinary was the way the lighting was captured. The house glowed in the painted sunset, making it special.

'It's good,' she said. 'Did you . . . ?'

'I did. I've never painted before, but suddenly this idea came into my head. It's based on a holiday cottage we went to as kids every summer. It's not too bad, is it?'

'It's not bad at all. In fact, it's very good.'

'I know I've a lot to learn about technique, but I'm excited about learning it.'

'Half the battle is enjoying what you're doing,' she said. 'I think you've got real potential.'

He looked so pleased she wanted to hug him. Then she remembered his girlfriend. The doorbell went downstairs and then came the sound of slightly raised voices. Before long, there was the clatter of high heels on the stairs, and when they both turned to the box room door, Karen was standing there. She looked furious. Kirsty's mouth opened and shut in astonishment. It was as if she'd conjured Karen up. But no, she was real enough, and she could almost feel the animosity radiating off her.

Alan couldn't believe it. What was Karen doing there? He'd made it perfectly clear that it was over between them. Although it was going to be awkward at work, he knew he'd be leaving soon anyway. It wasn't the kind of relationship that was going to easily morph into friendship, so he was surprised she was at his home. Not only that, but she seemed to think it entirely normal she should be there.

'I've been trying to get you on your mobile,' Karen said, ignoring Kirsty and pinning Alan with her frosty gaze.

'Sorry, the battery's drained and I haven't had a chance to charge it up. Why are you here?' he asked, knowing it was rude and abrupt but not caring.

The fact was, he'd been enjoying showing Kirsty his painting. He was enjoying having her here, and dinner had been a delight. It was a relief to be friends with someone, to feel relaxed with them and be able to have a laugh with no strings attached. He and Kirsty were simply friends. That was how it felt.

Splitting with Karen had been painful. She had made it so. Once Alan had made up his mind, he'd acted on it. But Karen didn't want to let go. She told him she wanted them to try to make a go of it. She wanted Alan to commit to his career as a lawyer, forget his crazy ideas, and for them to continue as a couple. She'd hinted on marriage, but above all, she told him they needed to concentrate on making money so they could get a large house, bigger cars and better lifestyles. She wanted to show the office how well she was doing despite not getting that promotion.

All of this had been water off a duck's back to Alan. He'd told her so. So why was Karen acting as if nothing had changed?

'It's the Graftons' drinks party tonight, darling. You haven't forgotten, have you?'

She gave a tinkling laugh that sounded so fake, Alan wanted to glance at Kirsty to see how she reacted.

'I told Tony and Caroline that we weren't coming,' he said.

'Oh, but we must go,' Karen said firmly. 'You do remember that Tony's portfolio is one of the largest our firm deals with. We can't avoid going. Get your jacket, darling, please.'

Now Alan did glance at Kirsty. She looked as confused as he felt. He didn't want to make an unpleasant scene in front of her, so he was relieved when she said she had to go.

'I'll drop you back,' he said.

'It's not a problem; I can get a taxi.'

'Let her get a taxi,' Karen interrupted. 'We're late as it is.'

Her blatant rudeness and disregard for Kirsty made something snap inside him. Up until then, he'd been willing to be civilised about their separation. After all, he was the one splitting them up. He'd put Karen's reactions down to a mix of hurt feelings and shock. Now, however, he was angry. She was selfish and inconsiderate. He'd always known she was driven by ambition. In the early days he'd liked that about her. Lately, that ambition was corroding any kindness in her.

'Please wait here a moment,' he said to Kirsty.

Then he took Karen firmly by her elbow and escorted her downstairs to the front door. She gaped at him, too surprised to speak.

'It's over,' he said. 'I'm sorry, but you have to understand that. We're not right for each other. I'm handing in my notice at the firm on Monday. You don't really want to marry a poor man, do you?'

She shuddered at that. 'Why are you

doing this? Why are you throwing it all away? Is it because of her?'

'Her? You mean Kirsty? She and I are just friends. No, this is about me, Karen. It's about what I want to do with my life. I'm sorry, but we want different things. I'm not the man you need.'

'You're right, I've had a lucky escape,' she sneered, turning to go. 'When you're living in a rented flat with no cash, don't come running to me to bail you out.'

She turned on her high heels and stormed away into the night.

7

'It was all a bit awkward,' Kirsty said. 'I felt like the proverbial gooseberry.'

She was at Lara's flat, having quickly freshened up at her own place after Alan dropped her off. She was telling Lara about being at Alan and Ian's house and how Karen had appeared.

Lara blew her nose and dumped the tissue into the bin, which was almost overflowing. Kirsty sighed and took it away to empty it in the larger kitchen bin. She brought another packet of paper tissues and tossed them on the bed before sitting again at her sister's side.

'Are they still together then?' Lara asked croakily.

Kirsty shrugged. 'I don't know. You could've cut the atmosphere with a knife. I don't know Alan well enough to ask. Anyway, how are you? You look awful.'

'Thanks,' Lara said, pulling a face. 'You really know how to boost my confidence.'

'Sorry, but you don't look at all well.'

'I'm getting better though. I hope to be back to school next week. I can't bear missing the last days in the run-up to the end of term. I hope my class have learnt their songs off by heart for the school show.'

Kirsty looked at Lara's bedside table. It was dominated by a large fruit basket, beautifully presented with pretty lilac cellophane wrap around it.

'Who sent you that?' She was slightly put out that she hadn't thought of bringing one herself. Instead, her offering was a couple of damp supermarket bags full of tins of soup, two bags of sliced bread and a jar of instant coffee.

Lara blushed. 'Ian brought it yesterday.'

'Did he, indeed?'

'Oh, don't be like that, he's just a friend you know. That's all.'

'He did look *very* friendly when he was asking me how you are,' Kirsty agreed with a grin. 'By the way, he's a decent cook, so when you two do finally get together, you won't starve.' She ducked the small pillow that came flying in her direction.

'Stop it,' Lara said. 'I mean it, Kirsty. You're totally wrong in that direction. I'm not interested in men, full stop.'

'Okay, but I think you're making a terrible mistake. Just because Mark was rubbish doesn't mean all men are. Ian seems lovely.'

'Seriously, can we stop it there?'

Lara had a fit of coughing. Kirsty leapt up and brought her a glass of water and the subject was dropped. *But not forever, Kirsty thought. No way. My little sister needs happiness, and Ian might be the man to provide it.* Someone had to show Lara that there were kind and good men out there in the big wide world.

'Mum phoned this morning to see how I am,' Lara said, sitting up straighter in her bed.

'And . . . ?' Kirsty said cautiously, sensing something else by Lara's tone.

'And apparently they've decided to go out to a restaurant for Christmas dinner. We're invited, obviously.'

'What? You're kidding!'

'No, I'm not. I told Mum you'd be very upset, but she says she and Dad have discussed it and it's what they want to do.'

'I'm going to go and see them. It's not right. We've never done that. We've always had a great family Christmas at home with the tree and presents and . . . and everything.' Kirsty was practically in tears. 'What's going on with them?'

'I wish I knew.' Lara shook her head. 'What I do know is that they need us. This is going to be a difficult Christmas.'

'I'll go over there right now,' Kirsty said, then halted. 'No, I can't. I've got my second date tonight. I'm meeting Ben at ten p.m. in the West End.'

'Ten? Isn't that rather late?'

'He doesn't finish work till nine, apparently. You'll approve of this one. He's an accountant.'

'Hmm, you know I don't approve of any of this. Please take care, promise me.'

'I'm more worried about our parents than I am about meeting dates right now. I'll go over and see them tomorrow. I can nip over at lunch time and shut up the shop for a bit.'

'I'd be glad if you did go and see them,' Lara said. 'I'd join you, but I'll probably still be in my bed.'

'I'm sure I can persuade them it's a crazy idea. I'll let you know how I get on. Now, what are your thoughts on what I should wear tonight? I want to look good for this accountant.'

Lara rolled her eyes. 'Please don't involve me in this. You say our parents are having a crazy idea over Christmas. Well, you doing online dating is even crazier, in my opinion.'

'That's sour grapes. You're just jealous you didn't think of it first. Can I borrow your new peach-coloured silk dress?'

This time she didn't manage to dodge the missiles. It ended in a fit of giggles for both sisters until Lara's coughing took over. Once Kirsty had helped by thumping her back, she headed home to get ready for her date.

★　★　★

The West End bar was surprisingly busy for a weekday evening. The music was jazz and blues, and the bar staff were friendly and attentive. Kirsty had found her date easily. He was quite attractive, she decided as they sat opposite each other in a booth next to the window. Ben had bought two glasses of wine and she sipped hers, feeling not too nervous. Not like last time with . . . what was his name again? She couldn't even remember. That was for

120

the best. She mustn't look backwards; instead, she must be enthusiastic for each date in case it was with The One.

'So Ben, how do you like being an accountant?' she said cheerily.

'Well, there's plenty to recommend it . . .'

She kind of zoned out while he explained the positives of his job. He had nice brown eyes and a strong, blunt jaw. His hair was thick and wavy. All in all, she liked what she saw. As for personality, as the evening went on, she liked that too. There was no immediate electric attraction; but, she reasoned, some relationships started with a slow burn and went on to become true love. So when Ben asked her if she'd like to meet him again, she said yes.

He looked taken aback.

Kirsty smiled. 'What? Did you think I'd say no?'

'You're a beautiful woman, and I guess I'm wondering why you need to meet potential partners online in the first place. I know why I do. I work such long hours I never meet anyone new. But why are you doing it?'

'Same reason — I never meet anyone either. Very few single men come shopping for Christmas in my shop,' she laughed.

She thought briefly of Alan. He certainly hadn't been single when he appeared in her shop. Was he single now? Even if he and Karen had split up, surely it was too soon for him to be looking for another relationship. Even if he did, she'd no indication that he liked her in that way. No, they were friends only. So she'd meet Ben for another date and see what happened. There was every possibility that when she met him again, she'd feel . . . more for him.

She waved goodbye to him at the train station and they parted. His train was going in the opposite direction. She was relieved at that. She wanted time to mull the evening over. It was a strain to keep conversation going with a complete stranger and to maintain a bright, cheerful manner. Alone in the carriage, she leant her head against the cold glass window.

If she could somehow feel the same spark of attraction for Ben that she felt each time she met Alan, wouldn't life be great? How simple it all would be! Then her thoughts drifted on to her parents and whatever was going on with them. Then there was Lara, seemingly stuck on a loop and unable to break free of what had happened with Mark and move on. She almost missed her stop, musing on it all.

The next morning she went into her shop early. It was time to do her Christmas shopping. She had some lovely merchandise this year and had mentally marked some items out, thinking of her family. Armed with a huge mug of coffee, she wandered round the shop for inspiration. Martha liked scented candles and Kirsty had a good stock of those. She selected a rose-scented candle with pressed rose petals in it. She'd already bought her mother a pair of warm knitted gloves in fuchsia-pink, one of the few presents she'd actually managed to get.

For Bob, she chose a chocolate selection box with the chocolates in Santa shapes. He liked old movies, so she opened up her laptop and ordered a box set of black and white classics. For Lara, she ordered up her favourite perfume. She'd noticed the bottle was low when she visited yesterday. It was expensive stuff. She left the laptop and went back out into the shop. She had just the gift to accompany the perfume. Carefully, she selected four of the glass angels on display and then tucked them into a box and wrapped it with paper and ribbons. Sorted.

She hesitated. Then she took a tin of toy soldiers from a shelf and wrapped them up. She took a set of bowls decorated with Christmas holly and crackers and wrapped those too. These gifts were a thank-you to Ian and William for their dinner last night. What about Alan? Aftershave or novelty chocolates? She didn't want to give anything too intimate, as if she was flirting with him. On the other hand, she didn't want to leave him out while giving gifts to his brother and nephew. In the end she opted for a book of Christmas quizzes. It was amusing and light-hearted and struck just the right note, she hoped.

At lunch time, after a busy morning of customers, she locked up the shop and headed for her parents' bungalow. She didn't miss the way Martha's face dropped when she saw who was at the front door.

'Darling, how lovely. Come on in. Dad's in the front room. He's injured his leg doing DIY.'

'Is he okay?' Kirsty rushed through to find Bob lying on the couch with his foot up.

'I'm fine,' he said. 'Your mother's fussing over me but it's a pulled muscle, nothing serious. Come and sit down with us. It's great to see you. How's business?'

'Busy, very busy. Anyway, the reason I'm here is — '

'Kirsty, can you give me a hand please?' Martha interrupted, leaning out from the kitchen door.

'Go on.' Bob waved her off. 'Bring me a nice cuppa, and I'll have one of Mum's homemade biscuits too.'

Once in the kitchen, Kirsty rounded on Martha. 'I know why you've pulled me in here, and it's not to make a pot of tea. How could you, Mum? How could you decide to go out to a restaurant on Christmas Day?'

'Darling, I was afraid you'd take it this way. I wanted to tell you personally, but I guess you heard it from Lara before I've had a chance to talk to you.'

'You could've phoned me.' She knew she sounded childish but was unable to stop.

Martha pulled out a kitchen chair and gently pushed her down onto it. Kirsty let her. Her eyes stung. If she wasn't careful, she'd end up blubbing like a baby. None of this was fair! They knew how much she loved a proper Christmas. So why were they doing it?

Martha sighed heavily. She sat down on another kitchen chair and Kirsty felt her mother's stare boring into her. She lifted her gaze and met it straight on. She wanted to know. Martha's gaze dropped first. She rubbed at her face and with a pang, Kirsty realised her Mum was tired.

She reached out and squeezed her mum's hand. 'Sorry, Mum. I don't mean to come across angrily, but I got a horrible shock when Lara told me. I don't understand. Can you explain why you and Dad have chosen this way to celebrate Christmas?'

'To be fair, it's not Dad's fault,' Martha said slowly. 'I'm the one to blame. Dad's quite happy to go along with whatever I want.'

'What does he want?'

'He would be fine with celebrating Christmas here. But I'm not. It's not Hambly. If we're breaking tradition by not being there on the day, then why not take it a step further and do it completely differently this year?'

Kirsty nodded. She got it. She really did. In a way, she agreed with her Mum. It was going to be sad not to be at Hambly. If they had Christmas in the new bungalow, they'd be constantly comparing it and finding it at fault. Perhaps the neutral territory of a restaurant was the answer.

They took their tea and biscuits back into the living room to sit with Bob. The situation with Christmas wasn't mentioned again. Kirsty chatted about her shop and how the business was doing. Martha and Bob, in turn, told her about the new loft insulation they'd had installed and how they'd been invited to their neighbours' for a New Year's Eve party.

Kirsty rushed back to the shop after lunch, still feeling disconcerted, and almost bumped into Alan, who was taking out rubbish to the roadside wheelies.

He watched as Kirsty ran up the

road. She hadn't seen him yet. A little surge of pleasure went through him at the sight of her. Her glossy brown hair bounced as she hurried along. Her bag was swinging madly and her skirts swished against her slim legs. She was like a small storm hurtling up the pavement.

'Hey, what's the hurry?' he called.

She looked up and gave him a wide smile. His heart lurched in his chest.

'Hey, yourself,' she said. 'I've been at my parents' for lunch and forgot the time. I hope I haven't lost any customers.'

'They all came into the gallery instead,' he said, wickedly.

'Oh.' Her face was dismayed.

'Not actually, but I've been busy enough. I also managed a quick trip to the hospital and I'm just back.'

'How's Simon?'

'He's improving all the time. In fact, the nurses say he'll be out for Christmas.'

'Oh, that's good news. Isn't it?'

Kirsty said, noticing Alan's frown.

He scratched the top of his head and grimaced. 'It is and it isn't. I've got a slight problem.'

'Do you want to talk about it?'

Somehow they'd moved into the gallery while chatting. Kirsty wondered why she felt so comfortable with him. Their movements and walking were so naturally in tune. Did he feel it too? There was no one in the gallery, which she was glad about. Whatever was worrying Alan, she wanted to be able to help him. He could speak freely without customers there to overhear.

'It's Karen,' he said. 'You met her yesterday. She and I . . . we've recently split up.'

'I'm sorry to hear that,' Kirsty said politely. Her heart leapt as she realised he was now officially single.

'We weren't right for each other. Anyway, the thing is . . . she's invited me, Ian and William to join her for Christmas in New York. She didn't take the break-up well and it's her way of making up for that, apparently. But now Uncle Simon's going to be coming home for Christmas, and I can't let the poor old chap come home to an empty house.'

'Can't you just say no to Karen?' Kirsty asked, thinking she'd be able to do so, no problem.

'It's not so simple. You see, she announced her kind offer in front of William. In a way, that was my fault. She phoned back last night and the phone was on loudspeaker, so he heard it all. He's so excited about going to New York, and I haven't the heart to disappoint him. He's had a bad time recently with the bullying and then moving school and so on.'

'So you already said yes to her?'

'Unfortunately, yes. Now I've found out Uncle Simon's coming home and I'm not at all sure what to do to please everybody. It looks like whatever I do, someone's going to be upset.'

'It sounds like our family Christmas this year.'

Alan listened while Kirsty explained about her parents' wish to go out to a restaurant for Christmas. The conversation moved on to other topics and he was in no hurry to get back to work for once. She told him an amusing story about her date the previous evening. Something burned in his chest momentarily. He was shocked to identify it as jealousy. Wow, where had that come from?

He and Kirsty were simply friends. Alan reminded himself of that fact. He said it inside his head three times for emphasis. Even if he did find her attractive, he wasn't going to ask her out. He'd been far too fast asking Karen out, and it had turned swiftly into a relationship. Look how that had ended. No, he thought firmly. He was going to take life slowly from now on. He was not going to date on the rebound. It would be a long while before he went on a date with anyone.

8

It was Sunday evening and Lara was watching soft fat snowflakes drifting down in the dark sky. The pale shapes were strangely mesmerising and soothing. She sipped her cup of hot orange juice and again felt grateful that her throat was no longer sore. In fact, she felt pretty good. The horrible cold was gone and she had some energy.

She picked up the phone to Moira Mellon. She wanted to get back to work and not miss the last week of school.

'Are you absolutely sure?' Moira asked at the other end of the line. 'We can manage without you. I've been covering your class and I can do so for another five days.'

'I'm feeling so much better,' Lara said. 'I want to come back tomorrow. I miss my little lot, and I do hope they're ready for the school nativity.'

'They've been practising like mad,' Moira assured her with a laugh. 'If enthusiasm counts for as much as talent, then I think we've got a winner on our hands. And to be honest, if you think you can manage it, I'd be very grateful. My emails are piling up and there are some meetings I need to hold before the end of term. So, see you tomorrow?'

'Yes, you will. I'll be in bright and breezy first thing,' Lara promised happily. 'Maybe I'll catch you for coffee at lunch break?'

'I look forward to it.'

Lara put the phone back in its holder with satisfaction. She was eager to get back to work and to make sure that this year's nativity was the best ever. Humming a little tune, she tidied up in the kitchen. She left the blinds up so that she could enjoy the snowflakes and put the radio on. Joyous Christmas carols filled the room. She was suddenly excited by the season. Maybe this was how Kirsty felt, she thought with a smile. There was so much to look forward to.

First, she'd have a week with her class and make sure the term ended on a high note for them. Then she'd have a lovely well-earned two weeks' holiday. Unlike Kirsty, she didn't mind too much that their Christmas meal was going to be in a restaurant. She wanted her parents to be content, and if going out on the special day meant that, then so be it. She hoped Kirsty would see that too. Kirsty in a grump wasn't a pretty sight.

She was mulling everything over and making mental lists when her doorbell rang. She jumped. She never got visitors on a Sunday evening. When she didn't immediately rush to open the flat door, there came a series of knocks, staccato and loud.

Concerned in case there was an emergency, she opened the door without looking through the peephole. Mark barged in, slamming the door behind him. Lara's hand flew to her chest in surprise.

'I knew you were in,' he said. 'Why didn't you answer the door?'

'Mark, what are you doing here?' Lara took a step back in the narrow hallway. It was a small flat and seemed suddenly tiny with Mark's large figure dominating the space.

'I've been to my counselling session and it was all about talking things through.'

'What, now? On a Sunday evening? Look, Mark, I don't think this is a good idea. It's late . . . it's snowing . . . I've got to get ready for school tomorrow.'

Mark shook his head. 'You're in denial, Lara. That's what that is. You should get some counselling too. In fact, I'll book you onto my course. It's very good, you'll learn a lot about yourself.'

Meanwhile, he'd pushed past her and was standing in her kitchen. It was Lara's favourite room. She'd painted it a lovely buttercup yellow and bought blond wood furniture. Her everyday crockery was blue and white striped and she had a china hen for her eggs. It was unashamedly a farmhouse kitchen style, and she loved it.

Seeing Mark in it was an intrusion. He didn't belong there. He didn't belong in her life at all. But how was she to get rid of him? If only she had the guts to stand up to him. But he was a good foot taller than her. It wasn't as if she could physically push him out of her flat. She had to somehow persuade him to leave.

Lara took a long, silent breath. It filled her lungs and eased the constriction in her chest. 'Please go, Mark,' she said, quietly.

He stared at her with a curl of his lip as if he disliked her. Lara's heart beat painfully against her ribs. He wasn't going to go. She had a terrible feeling about him.

'You said you'd go for a drink with me,' Mark said. 'Why don't we have one here instead? What have you got? I'll have a beer.' He sauntered over to her fridge and peered in.

There was plenty in her fridge, thanks to Kirsty and Ian. She had eggs and milk and cheeses. There was a well-stocked veg box with courgettes, corn and a butternut squash. She even had a tinfoil tray of chicken curry which Ian had made and brought a portion for her. There was no beer.

Mark made an exasperated noise at the back of his throat. 'Any wine, then?'

'I've been ill, I haven't had a glass of wine for days.'

'You don't look ill to me. Been skiving off work, have we?'

'Look, I'll make you a cup of tea and we can talk for a little bit, but not too long, okay?' Lara said feebly.

She hated herself. If Kirsty was here, she'd have got rid of Mark easily. There was no pushing her sister around. Then she thought of Ian. She glanced back into the hall where the phone sat on its stand. Maybe she could phone him. Mark sat heavily and indicated the chair opposite. Lara sat. She couldn't reach the phone now. She'd have to go through this. Whatever it was going to be.

'The session I was at on Friday was all about communicating. I'd have come and seen you Friday or Saturday about it but I was busy.'

No mention of whether it would have been convenient for her, Lara noted. Everything was still all about Mark. Despite the counselling, he couldn't see that. It was as if the world reflected him. He'd no empathy for others. She knew that for certain. She'd put up with it for two long years. Inside, a little flicker of anger was growing. It was an unusual emotion for Lara to experience.

'The point is, we'd never have broken off our engagement if we'd talked to each other more,' Mark said.

'You never wanted to discuss much,' Lara said.

She was thinking of the major decisions they should have had together when they were engaged but hadn't because Mark refused to. He'd told her he would make the final decision on when and where they got married and where they lived afterwards. That had been the final straw for Lara. It had taken his extreme arrogance on the matter of their wedding and future together for her to leave him.

'The trouble with you is that you're too indecisive,' Mark said. 'You needed me to make the decisions.'

Was that true? She was shaken by this accusation, made so matter-of-factly. She did like to think things through carefully. But she could make decisions. Even if they were trodden over by Mark.

'I don't need you now,' Lara said, standing up and gripping the edge of the kitchen table for support. The hard wood felt comforting under her palms. She pressed down, anchoring herself. She visualised Kirsty as she spoke to Mark with more courage than she felt. 'You have to leave now.'

'I haven't finished.' He deliberately sat back in the chair, legs wide as if he'd sit there all night and there wasn't one thing she could do to prevent it.

Lara's pulse raced. For a very long moment they stared at each other. Mark's expression was smug with something darker roaming in his eyes. Lara felt weak, as if her fever was returning. In the silence, the doorbell rang once; twice. Mark swore. Lara fled along the short hallway and pulled the door open, half-expecting Mark's hands on her shoulders tearing her back.

She almost burst into tears to see Ian and William standing there. Ian had a smile on his face which faltered when he saw her distress.

'Are you okay? Is this a bad time?'

'No, no, please come in.'

Mark thundered down the hall and pushed rudely past them.

'Hey!' Ian shouted after him.

They heard the heavy clatter of his feet on the stairwell and the outside door slam. Lara led them into the kitchen. William hopped up onto the chair and sat, kicking his feet and looking about with interest. Ian gazed at her in concern.

'What was all that about?' he asked.

'That was my ex-fiancé trying to communicate,' she said shakily.

'Communicate?'

'It's a long story,' she sighed.

'This is the same guy who's hanging about at the school gates every day waiting for you?' Ian said, and she heard the worry in his voice.

'Yes, that's Mark. He can't seem to let me go.'

'Have you told the police?' Ian said.

'No, it's not that bad. Mark . . . well, he's selfish, I guess. He's working stuff through in counselling, so I should be glad of that.'

'He's a bully,' William said, 'isn't he, Lara?'

She nodded. 'He is a bully. But you told me I have to stand up to him, so I'm trying to do that.'

Although she'd failed miserably

tonight. What would she have done if Ian hadn't turned up? She didn't want to think about it.

'If he keeps bothering you, let me know,' Ian said.

'Thanks.'

A warmth flooded her. She wasn't alone. It was reassuring that tall, broad-shouldered Ian was on her side. She looked at William and smiled. 'What brings you two here? It's lovely to see you both.'

William flicked a nervous glance at his dad. Ian took a deep breath. He ruffled William's hair before speaking.

'We need your help,' he said.

'My help?' She'd been thinking of how they'd helped her. It was a surprise to know they needed her.

'William doesn't want to go to school tomorrow,' Ian said.

William stared at his fingers as if they were the most interesting objects he'd ever seen.

'That's a shame,' she said, 'because

I'm going back to school tomorrow. I'll miss you.'

William raised round eyes to her.

'Oh, and I'm sorry I haven't been able to be there for William after school,' Lara said to Ian. 'How have you been managing?'

'I've juggled meetings. It's been fine, honestly. It was far more important that you got your strength back. You look better. You must be better if you're going back to work.'

Lara got up and found some biscuits in her cupboard. She slid them onto a plate and put the kettle on. She set the biscuits in front of William and got orange juice. She poured him a tall glass. The actions gave her time to think. How was she to help William back to school?

'So why don't you want to go to school tomorrow?' she asked casually, as if she didn't care what he answered.

He picked at a fingernail. Then, when she didn't say anything else, he took a biscuit and nibbled it all round the edge. Ian got up and took two mugs from the mug tree. Lara pushed the tea caddy over to him. She understood he was giving his son room to speak without pressure. They shared an anxious smile. It felt oddly natural, having Ian in her kitchen. Almost as if they were a couple. Lara squashed that rebel thought.

'Ben's off sick,' William said finally. 'He got your cold and he's not been in class all week.'

'What about Lucy? I thought she was your friend too.'

William shook his head sadly. 'Lucy's playing with Emily. She says Emily's her best friend, not me.'

Lara could picture it quite easily. The dynamics of the friendships had shifted. It happened all the time in the class. William was too young to realise that they could shift back just as quickly. Lara bet as soon as Ben was better, the friendship would resume as if nothing had changed. It was convincing William that was the challenge.

'I'd keep him home,' Ian said, 'but I've got a client meeting in the south tomorrow. I'll be away early and won't be home till late. Alan can take him to school and probably pick him up, but I can't ask him to have William all day at the gallery.'

Lara knew from her teaching experience that it wasn't a good idea giving in to school refusing. If parents gave in once, then they found it a whole lot harder to get their child back into school subsequently.

'You know, William, I've got a problem too,' she said.

She stared at her fingers just the way he'd been doing. William finished his biscuit and stared at her curiously. She felt Ian's gaze on her too.

'What problem?'

'I'm a bit worried about going back to school tomorrow too. I've been off all week and Mrs Mellon has been teaching the class, as you know. I've missed all the singing practice for the show and I don't know if I'll catch up. I don't know what lessons Mrs Mellon's been giving you.'

'I can help you,' William piped up excitedly. 'I know what lessons we've done. I can show you my jotters. And . . . and I can sing you the songs. I know them all. Mrs Mellon said I did very well.'

'When can I see your jotters?'

'Tonight,' he said. 'You can come to our house and see them. Can't she, Dad?'

'It's far too late, William. It's past your bedtime and Lara needs to rest,' Ian said, catching on to what Lara was doing. He winked at her behind William's back.

'Well . . . ' William paused, his brow furrowed in thought. 'I suppose I could come to school early tomorrow and show you them.'

'That would be lovely,' Lara said. 'Would you really do that for me? I thought you weren't going to go to school.'

'I'll do it to help you,' William said

bravely. Then, after a moment, 'Do you think Ben will be at school?'

'I hope so,' she said. 'If not, you can be my special helper all day.'

As it was getting late, Ian and William left soon after. Lara yawned. Definitely time for bed. Especially as she'd need to get up early to pack her school bag. She went to put down the blinds. The snow was still falling and the ground was covered in a shallow white quilt. Her fingers froze on the cord. Under the street light opposite was Mark. As Ian's car pulled out from the curb and drove off, Mark turned to watch it go. She saw his face in the LED lighting, plainly lit. It was contorted with anger.

* * *

Further away in the new residential development, Martha was also watching the snow. She stared out through the patio doors, glad to be inside in the warmth of her living room. The snow covered the tiny lawn and lay like a muffler on top of the privet hedge. On the other side, in the neighbours' garden, there were sparkling lights, blue and red, glistening. They cheered up the surroundings and gave a festive feel to the area.

Bob hobbled up behind her. His leg had not yet healed. 'What are you looking at, love?'

'I'm admiring Dennis and Anya's garden lights. Aren't they pretty?' Martha said.

'Dennis and Anya. So you've met the neighbours on that side, then. It's the other side that have invited us for the New Year's party, is it?'

'Yes, dear. It's Graeme and Betty on that side over there who are holding the party. I believe Dennis and Anya will be going to it, so you'll have a chance to meet them then. I got talking to them over the garden hedge. One of the benefits of a small garden. Our neighbours at Hambly were never visible, the gardens were so large.'

Bob put his arm around her and

squeezed her shoulders affectionately.

'Sounds as if there are some positives to the new house, eh?'

Martha poked him in the ribs playfully. 'All right, I admit it. It has its ups as well as downs. But I still miss Hambly.'

'We all do, love. It's not just you.' There was a gentle reproof in her husband's voice.

Martha realised she'd been selfish. She'd wallowed in her own unhappiness. She'd forgotten that Bob was adjusting to their new life as well. It was just that he'd seemed to adjust much easier. She'd resented that.

'And I still want to go out for Christmas dinner,' she said quickly.

Bob nodded. 'We'll do whatever you want. I don't mind.'

'Kirsty does.'

'Kirsty wears her heart on her sleeve. She'll get over it. Who knows, she might even enjoy it, going out to a posh restaurant for a slap-up meal.'

'When you put it like that, it sounds

rather good,' Martha laughed. 'I hope you're right. Kirsty can be obstinate, as we know. At least Lara won't mind.'

'That's a safe bet. She's a good influence on her sister, so I'm sure they'll both be fine, whatever we decide to do.'

Later, when Bob had gone to bed to rest his leg, Martha wandered around tidying up. She picked up some magazines that Bob had been reading beside the sofa. They were open at the travel pages. She read some of the deals. They were accompanied by pictures of glorious aquamarine seas and white sands and sun, sun, sun. She sighed, then frowned. Why was Bob reading them? Slowly Martha smiled. Perhaps Bob wasn't as set in his ways as she'd thought. She'd have another chat with him tomorrow about holidays. She set the magazines in a neat stack and turned off the living room lights. Then she made her way to bed.

9

'And don't forget, if you run out of boxes of crackers, I've got loads more in the back store room.'

'Yes, dear. You already told me that,' Martha said.

'Did I? Did I really? I must be losing it. Anyway, Mum, I'm warning you, it's going to be awfully busy if it's anything like recent days,' Kirsty said.

They were in the Christmas shop, behind the counter. The countertop was frothing with curled ribbons and tissue paper in every hue imaginable. Martha worked one day a week in the shop, which allowed Kirsty a day to do the stock take and the books and general admin. But today she was playing hooky and meeting Ben for lunch.

'Is he a nice young man?' Martha asked again, tidying up the tissue and rewinding the ribbons neatly.

'Who?'

'This man you're meeting for lunch. Is he nice?'

'Oh, Ben, you mean. Yes, he seems very nice. We had a lovely date last time in a really hip bar. He had plenty to say for himself — has all his own teeth and a fine thick head of hair. What more could a woman ask for?'

'Kirsty,' Martha warned, 'be serious. Do you really think this online dating thing is working out?'

Kirsty wrinkled her nose in thought. Absent-mindedly, she pulled out the ribbons from the case that Martha had just replaced them in. Her mother sighed inwardly and bit her lip.

'Yes! It's . . . it's fine.'

'You don't sound very sure, dear. How about trying to meet nice young men in the normal way?'

'How? Tell me that, Mum. How?' Kirsty splayed her arms and spun round, encompassing her shop. 'Do you see any gorgeous single men here? No, you don't. That's why I have to use the Apple Tree Blossom site.'

'Great name,' Martha remarked, once more rolling up the ribbons and making sure they were out of her daughter's reach. 'I just wonder . . . if it's *right*, somehow.'

'Times have moved on since you and Dad met.'

'I'm not sure they have. Look at Lara and Mark. They met on a romantic cruise.'

'Bad example.'

Martha sighed. 'Yes, it was. Silly me. But I'm sure I can think of a hundred other examples where it's worked out very happily. For example, your cousin Claire and her Rennie.'

'Now that was romantic,' Kirsty agreed with a dreamy smile. 'She falls off an elephant in Thailand and he catches her before she hits the ground. Great wedding too, on the beach in Thailand where they first met. That was wonderful, wasn't it?'

Martha nodded. 'Even your father

enjoyed that trip.'

'How is Dad?'

'His leg is improving. He's been looking at travel offers, which is exciting. I haven't quite broached the subject; I'll wait till after Christmas. But I'm fairly certain there's a cruise in my future somewhere.'

'You deserve a holiday. You didn't have one this summer because of getting rid of Hambly.'

'Getting rid of Hambly. Oh, when you put it like that, it sounds awful.'

'Look, Mum, I'm not going to pretend I'm glad we sold our home. But I suppose we all have to move on. Move forward. For me, that's making my shop a success and finding love at some point, I hope. For you and Dad it must be being happy post-Hambly.'

'We're working on that,' Martha said.

'About Christmas . . .'

'Oh, not that again. Aren't you going to be late for your lunch?'

Kirsty glanced hastily at her watch. Her mother was right; she had to go.

But there was something she needed to say before she went.

'I had an idea. About Christmas. One that doesn't include a restaurant.'

Kirsty watched her mother carefully. To give Martha credit, she didn't blast her down immediately. Instead, she put on a polite smile and gave Kirsty the floor, so to speak.

'I thought . . . maybe, instead of going out for a meal in a sterile location, we could change Christmas in a different way.'

'What do you mean?'

'How about inviting some other people to join us? We've never done that. We've always had our own family Christmas and then socialised at New Year.'

'It would be different,' Martha said. 'Who did you have in mind?'

'Simon and his nephews. Alan is running the gallery next door while Simon is in hospital. Alan's brother, Ian, is very nice and he has a cute kid called William. Simon's coming home before Christmas. There's a slight complication in that they might be going to New York; but if that doesn't pan out, I thought . . . I thought we could invite them over.'

Martha paused. Kirsty saw her mother's fingers cease their sorting. The ribbons were fully packed. The tissue paper was neatly folded, square and smooth, ready for action. She kept her fingers crossed and her breath held.

'I'll think about it,' Martha said finally. 'Now, are you going to meet this Ben person, or aren't you?'

Kirsty grabbed her bag and kissed her mother, smack on the cheek. 'I love you, Mum. Don't ever forget that.'

Then she was running towards the station at full tilt. The next train to the city was due in five minutes and she did not want to miss it.

*　　*　　*

Ben had given her directions to the tapas restaurant. It was in a cobbled side street in a trendy part of the city. Until recently, it had been a run-down area with empty shop fronts and shabby flats. Now, vegetarian cafés, community arts centres and a diverse range of eateries had mushroomed up and the flats were becoming rather expensive to buy or rent. Kirsty liked the old-town look of the place and she loved tapas. She decided she liked Ben more and more. It was the kind of restaurant she might well have chosen herself. *In fact*, she thought, *I'll pick the venue for our next date*. This gave her a little thrill. She was bold enough to feel there might be a next date. Perhaps an evening at the cinema followed by a meal? Or was it too soon to invite him home to meet her parents?

She went into the tapas restaurant, feeling high-spirited. She put aside her worries about Christmas and her parents, Lara and Mark and her own state of singledom. After all, it looked like that was about to end. She thought briefly about Alan, then put him from her mind. He'd only just split up from Karen. And . . . he'd never asked Kirsty out or given any hint that he thought of her as anything but a friend. She had to be content with that.

Ben waved her over. He was wearing a light grey jacket over jeans and a white T-shirt. He looked great. The outfit went well with his dark wavy hair, and she noticed his cute fashionable stubble.

'Hey,' he greeted her.

'Hey, yourself,' she said casually, sliding into the seat opposite him and feeling good. There was a wonderful aroma of garlic and tomato and other spicy flavours in the air. The place was buzzing with the customers' conversations, and several waiting staff flowed through the room efficiently with silver platters of tapas.

'It's great to see you again,' Ben said with a perfect white grin.

Kirsty waited to feel something. It was strange. She could quite appreciate how handsome Ben was in an observant, logical way. But she couldn't *feel* it, deep down in her stomach or running along her nerves. What on earth was wrong with her? Here she was, having a lunch date with the most gorgeous guy possible, and she might as well have been dining with her granny!

This won't do, she told herself. *I have to work at this*. So she put herself out to be the most entertaining companion possible over lunch. She told jokes and funny stories until Ben was laughing out loud. They both chose dishes to share. Ben told her that her choices were amazing. She told him he was amazing too for choosing her favourites — garlic sizzling prawns, sautéed potatoes and fried whitefish.

After the first course, they ordered ice-cream and coffee. Kirsty was beginning to feel happy. Okay, she didn't fancy Ben perhaps as much as she should. But that would come in time, she was sure of it. Besides, she must feel something for him. She'd turned down other dates in the meantime, since she'd met him. That had to count for something, right? She was prepared to see him exclusively. Who knew, after a few dates she'd probably realise he was The One. Wouldn't she?

'Do you know how cute you are when you're thinking?' Ben said.

'Am I?'

'Sure. Your forehead gets all wrinkled and your eyes darken.'

'That sounds quite awful. I don't want to be all wrinkly.'

'You aren't, chill out. You've got wonderful skin, which I'm sure you know.'

Kirsty felt a bit annoyed. Of course she knew she wasn't wrinkly. She'd meant that as a joke. Instead, it sounded like she was fishing for compliments. She'd had a couple of glasses of white wine with lunch. She wasn't focusing as sharply as usual. She looked at Ben. His stubble suddenly looked less glamorous and more like he hadn't bothered to shave. She noticed a speck of tomato sauce on his white T-shirt. He sniffed and the sound irked her.

She caught herself. *Stop being so critical.* What was wrong with her?

'How's your work?' she said, hoping to change the subject.

'Actually, it's awful. My boss is useless and I'm fed up.'

'I thought you liked your job. You told me all about how marvellous accountancy is when we met up last time.'

Ben sighed. 'Let's face it, we both put on our best fronts, didn't we? Of course we did. First dates and all that.' He shrugged. 'Well, now I'm telling you the truth. I hate my job.'

Kirsty swallowed the last scoop of her ice-cream and washed it down with coffee. The music in the room began to jar on her ears. Or was it Ben's whining as he described his latest meeting with his boss?

She was prepared to overlook all that. Of course some people hated their jobs and their bosses. She was extremely lucky to work for herself. Lara was lucky that she loved her job and liked working for Moira Mellon. A lot of people had it otherwise. She was just a bit surprised how Ben had changed his tune.

'I wouldn't have minded if you'd told me the truth the first time we met,' she said.

He shook his head. 'No, you would have. You'd have refused to meet me again. Let's be honest, we all want some magic, we all think we're going to meet the perfect partner, if we only try hard enough. Well, that was me trying hard.'

'It's okay,' Kirsty said, 'I like you the way you are. You don't have to try so hard.'

'Believe me, you're in the minority. Since we met, I've dated four other girls and I'm pretty sure they expect the fantasy me, not the real me.'

'You're dating other women?' Kirsty asked, dismayed.

'Yeah, we're not exclusive. Hey, we never said that, did we? It's statistical. The more you date, the more chance you're going to find the partner of your dreams. Kirsty? Kirsty!'

Kirsty was already standing, her coat on, fumbling for her purse. She put down her share of the bill on the table. She didn't want to be beholden in any way to him.

'Thanks for lunch, Ben. I don't think we'll be seeing each other anymore.'

She paused. He looked confused. 'What's the matter?'

'Nothing, not really. It's me, not you.' Kirsty couldn't begin to explain what she meant. Only . . . she had honestly thought Ben and she could have had something good going. So much for planning for the cinema. She'd even, in her mind, picked out a couple of good films to see!

★ ★ ★

Her shop window was brightly lit and enticing. She stared into it, not seeing the window display, just her miserable face staring back. She hesitated, ready to push the door open and go in. Then she glanced next door to the gallery. Instinctively, she moved along the pavement and pushed open the gallery door. Her mother could manage without her for a little longer.

A gush of lovely warm air greeted her. She shut the door behind her to keep out the winter chill. 'Alan?' she called.

He appeared from the back room and her heart thumped loudly. Could he hear it? A flush spread across her face.

'Kirsty, good to see you. Come on in; you look frozen.'

Good — he'd clearly taken her flushed face for frostbite! Kirsty allowed him to guide her to the chairs. There was a mass of tinsel on the floor along with plastic baubles, a knot of coloured lights and a sad-looking tree lying on its side on the polished floor.

'What's going on?' she said, taking off her coat and enjoying the lovely warmth of the room.

'Oh, decorating the gallery. It's about time, isn't it?' Alan said cheerfully.

Why, oh why, did the sight of his face spark her nerves and send a tingle right through her ribcage? Why couldn't Ben's equally handsome features do likewise? She shut her eyes tightly for a moment. Then she blinked them open to try again. She saw Alan's frown.

'You okay? Got a headache?'

'Headache? Oh, no, not at all. Shall I help you put these up?' she said, embarrassed.

'That'd be great. What do you think of the tree? I found it upstairs in the storeroom, but some of the branches are bent — it's plastic.'

'I'm sure we can restore them,' Kirsty said, kneeling down at the tree to assess it. Suddenly she felt completely comfortable. It was so easy being with Alan. He was good company and she enjoyed it.

'If you're sure about that, then let me lift it upright.'

She was all too aware of him as he brushed by her and lifted up the tree. She liked the way his broad shoulder muscles filled out his shirt. She liked the way he had long legs, lean in faded jeans. She liked the way his fair hair grew and the tiny wave in it.

'Kirsty?'

'Hmmm? What?'

'I said, do you want to put the baubles on it?' He sounded amused.

'Sorry, yes I do.'

'Hold that then, and I'll go and get a couple of weights to keep it upright.'

She was left holding the tree. She pushed it slowly into the corner, where the walls could help prop it up. Then she managed to bend one of the plastic boughs back into position without snapping it. A small success, but a satisfying one. More satisfying than her date today. Kirsty sighed. She was deep in her not very happy musings when she became aware of Alan behind her.

'Look what I found in one of the boxes.'

She turned, almost bumping into his broad chest. 'Sorry,' she mumbled.

Then she saw what he was holding. It was mistletoe. Real mistletoe. She looked up at him. His face was suddenly so close to hers. She saw the shape of his lips. Saw the faint shadow of his stubble. No designer there, just rugged male. His jaw was firm and blunt. She smelt his faint fragrance of soap and clean cotton with a hint of spice.

Without thought, her face tilted up to his. She imagined their feather-light touch of his lips, deepening and firm.

Alan coughed. Kirsty jumped. He stood back with the mistletoe hanging from his fingers.

'I'll go and put this somewhere,' he muttered, not meeting her gaze.

'Good idea,' she said, slightly dazed.

Had she imagined the whole thing? She watched him hang up the plant and then put up decorations. He was strangely quiet, as if he couldn't bear to speak to her. She grabbed her abandoned coat and put it on.

'I've got to go,' she said. He nodded and didn't try to stop her.

Kirsty hurried next door. She didn't go into her shop but ran upstairs to her flat and slammed the door behind her. Then she ran into her bedroom and sat on her bed.

She was in love with Alan. The knowledge of it hit her hard.

It was true. She loved him. She let the words swirl deliciously around her head. No wonder she wasn't attracted to Ben. No wonder she'd turned down other dates. She wasn't interested in the myriad of men out there in the big, wide world. No. She had found her other half, the man who completed her, right next door.

The only trouble was, he didn't seem to feel the same way about her.

Kirsty made herself a cup of tea. Then she went to her laptop and unsubscribed from the Apple Tree

Blossom website. There was no point wasting her time on more dates. She wished Ben well in his search for his soulmate. She even wished Adrian well, and hoped he found a girlfriend who appreciated model railways. There was supposed to be someone for everyone, somewhere in the world, so she reckoned he'd find her eventually. As for Kirsty, she'd have to wait until Alan got over Karen and discovered he liked small, dark-haired, impulsive women.

If, indeed, that ever happened.

10

Where, oh where was her briefcase? Lara gulped down her hot tea and winced. She hadn't done her makeup; hadn't yet brushed her hair and put it up. And, worst of all, she'd mislaid her bag with all her lesson plans. She'd missed her alarm clock ringing this morning, and her normally to-the-minute schedule was now all out of kilter. She couldn't be late for work. She just couldn't!

Moira had been so grateful to see her back at school. Lara, in turn, was grateful to her head teacher for keeping her class on track. She'd been able to slide easily back into lessons and noted that all her pupils were doing well. William had turned up for class, and Lara was relieved to see that Ben was back at school too and the two boys were happy to see each other. At the first break time, she saw that Lucy and Emily had joined them. With any worry about William out of the way, Lara's main problem was her class's singing lessons until the school show.

Ten minutes later, she was clattering downstairs, car keys in hand. There was no time to walk to school today. Her hair was twisted up in a stylish bun and her makeup was applied. She'd found her briefcase behind a pile of laundry that was a day behind being washed. At least the end of term was in sight, she thought. Then she'd have two clear weeks to organise herself. Her horrible cold had thrown her into disarray, which was very unlike her. She caught herself wondering about Christmas Day and then made herself stop. She'd think about it later and phone Kirsty to see what the latest update with their parents was.

Lara unlocked her car door, threw her briefcase and handbag onto the passenger seat, and buckled into the driver's side. She started the engine and began to pull out from the curb.

A horrible grinding and flapping noise reverberated in the enclosed space. What on earth? She turned the ignition off and got out.

She gave a cry of dismay. Her front tyres were completely flat. She bent down for a closer look. The tyres had been slashed. Lara straightened up, her heart thumping. She glanced about. She remembered Mark's fury the other night, so visible under the street lighting. Was he here? Was he watching her right now?

She grabbed her handbag and fumbled for her mobile with trembling fingers. Without conscious thought, she pressed Ian's number.

'Hello? Lara?'

'Ian, thank goodness.' Lara stepped away from the curb onto the broad pavement with its sturdy trees. She kept her back to the nearest tree trunk and her eyes fixed along the road, searching for her ex-fiancé.

'Are you all right?'

'I need a favour. My car's out of action and I'm going to be late for work. Is there any chance you could give me lift, please?'

'I'll be with you in five minutes.'

The line clicked off. She slid the mobile into her pocket, where she could grab it quickly. Not for the first time, she was thankful to have Ian as a friend. She hated having to ask him to pick her up, but ever so glad he was able to.

Within a few minutes, his dark blue car drew up. He jumped out. 'How did that happen?' he said when he saw the tyres.

'I don't know,' Lara said, not wanting to discuss it or even think about what it meant. 'Thanks so much for coming to get me. I'm going to be late . . . '

'Of course. Come on, I'll get you to school. I've just dropped William there.'

'I'm so sorry to be a bother.'

Ian glanced over at her with a warm smile as they drove off. 'You're never that. I'm glad you thought to phone me.'

Lara smiled back at him.

'Was it Mark?'

'Yes, I'm sure of it. The tyres were cut deliberately. I think he's angry about the other evening when you arrived and he stormed out.'

'Lara . . . it's none of my business, I know that, but I really think you need to go to the police with this.'

'Oh, no, I don't want to do that. I don't want any trouble.' Lara gripped her bags.

'You've already got trouble,' Ian said gently.

He indicated left and turned the corner to the school. He parked up, and the car was suddenly quiet as the engine purred to a stop. They sat for a moment. Lara knew she should go. The school bell rang out insistently. Nine o'clock and the start of the school day. But she was frozen to the seat.

'At least tell me where Mark lives,' Ian said.

'Why?'

'Don't worry, I'm not going to do

anything. I just want to go and talk to him. Persuade him that this has to stop. He has to stop harassing you and realise it's over between you.'

'You don't have to do that for me,' Lara said, turning to him. 'It's very kind, but Mark can be . . . I don't want you to get hurt.'

'I promise it won't come to that.'

They still sat there. Lara knew she should be hurrying towards her classroom. Ian waited patiently.

'All right,' she said finally. 'Mark's house is out of town, along the Compton Road, number twenty. I've got to go. Thanks for the lift.'

She didn't look back. She had the awful feeling that if she did, she'd burst into tears. Ian was right; the situation with Mark was getting out of hand. She could handle him turning up to speak to her. Just. But vandalising her car was a step up from that. A line had been crossed. Ian was probably right that she should call the police. But Lara shrank from that; it made her problem official.

Not only that, but she was sure it would enrage Mark further.

★　★　★

Ian watched Lara walk quickly across the school playground and waited until she was safely indoors before driving away. Although he had an inbox full of work that morning, he drove straight over to Compton Road. He watched number twenty for a few minutes. He didn't know whether Mark was at home. Did he have a job? Lara hadn't said. She hadn't said much about her ex-fiancé in general. But Ian had seen enough of the man to find him obnoxious. The question was whether he was also dangerous.

A shadow passed behind the curtains in the lower window of the flat. Someone was there. Ian took a deep breath. He'd been completely honest with Lara when he said he simply wanted to talk to Mark. He'd no intention of having a fight. Ian was no coward, but he abhorred violence. In his opinion, it had never solved the world's problems.

He thought back to the incident when he might have happily hit Mark after he'd muddied up Lara's jotters. Ian shook his head. Okay, he wasn't perfect. He needed to keep his temper in check. He got out of the car.

The front garden to number twenty was untidy, with straggling grasses and a couple of empty crisp packets. The road formed part of the route to the high school, and Ian imagined slouching sixth-formers throwing their litter carelessly over the low wall. Mark clearly hadn't bothered to clear them up.

He rang the bell. Already adrenaline was running through his system. He tried to keep calm. The door opened. Mark stared out with a hostile glare.

'If you're selling something, I don't want it.' He began to shut the door.

'Wait.'

'I know you, don't I?' Mark said

slowly. 'You're the guy who's been hanging around Lara.'

I could say the same about you. Ian didn't answer that. Instead, he said, 'Lara is a friend of mine.'

'*A friend*, is she,' Mark sneered. 'You keep away from her. Lara's mine.'

Ian bristled at Mark's tone and possessiveness. 'Lara doesn't belong to anyone but herself,' he said quietly.

'What do you want?'

'I want to ask you if there's any reason I shouldn't phone the police about your behaviour.'

Ian watched Mark turn visibly pale. 'I don't know what you're talking about. Are you threatening me?' he blustered.

'We both know that you slashed Lara's car tyres. I'm pretty sure that the CCTV along her street will have picked you up.'

Mark turned a shade whiter. He didn't appear to have shaved that morning, and there were dark circles under his eyes. Ian almost felt sorry for him. Then he thought of what Lara had

had to put up with from this man and his heart hardened.

'What's it to you?' The question sounded genuinely as if Mark was puzzled about Ian's angle.

'As I said, Lara is a good friend, and I don't like to see her upset. There are two options. Either I go to the police and tell them about the damage to her car, or you promise to keep away from her. Which is to be?'

Mark stared at him, eyes glittering. Ian stood his ground. The primitive part of his brain was taking in information. Mark's height and breadth compared to his own. The angle of the door, should it slam. Mark's body language. It seemed to him that they were both tense. Certainly, his own muscles were tightened and ready. The age-old fight-or-flight reaction was in place.

Suddenly, Mark's body slumped. It was as if he'd given up. He rubbed one large hand over his jaw, and Ian heard the rasping sound of his unshaven skin.

'You love her too. That's what this is. I'm right, aren't I? I've been trying to win her back and I've lost to you.'

'I'm her friend, that's all.' How many times did he have to repeat himself?

'Yeah, right.' Mark's voice dripped with sarcasm. 'And I'm Father Christmas.'

'You won't win her back by intimidating her, that's certain,' Ian said.

'Are you going to phone the police? I'll lose my job if that happens.'

'Then you choose the alternative and leave Lara alone.'

'I don't *have* a choice, do I? You've got it all sewn up. You've won.'

Mark took a step back inside his flat and slammed the door. Ian jumped back smartly. His body was still on high alert as he walked back to his car. He imagined Mark's eyes boring into his back. But when he looked at the window, there was nothing. He was glad to get into his car. Mark's words echoed in his brain as he headed home. *You love her too.*

At home, Ian made a pot of tea and carried it through to his work desk. His inbox had picked up another fifteen emails in his absence, all work-related. His mobile had several messages too, about new projects as well as from existing clients. He couldn't afford to take an hour off to think about things. He slung his coat over the back of his chair and clicked the mouse to wake up his spreadsheets screen.

The realisation of it washed over him like a stream in torrent. He did love Lara. He was in love with her. He didn't want to be just a good friend. He wanted her in his life, wanted her beside him every day.

Ian blew out a breath of surprise. Then he knew he'd do nothing about it. How could he? He was no one's knight in shining armour. He came with a whole lot of baggage. He still loved his wife, and he had a little boy who needed him more than anyone else did. Lara had her own complications in the form of Mark. Ian doubted Mark would be able to keep his word about staying away from her. It wasn't that, though. He wasn't sure if Lara was over her ex-fiancé. Why else did she let him visit her? Why was she so adamant she didn't want the police involved?

No, it was better for both of them if Ian kept his emotions hidden. Besides, how would William take it if he decided to remarry? Ian shook his head, his mouth firm. He opened up his emails and clicked on the first message, blocking out all thoughts except those related to architecture.

* * *

Martha hadn't had a moment to ask Bob about the travel brochures. The snow had mostly gone now, leaving grubby grey lumps of it in the street and on the paths. She'd scraped most of it off with a spade from their garden. It was odd how fond she'd become of their new garden. She liked that it was easy to look after, being so small. Now she hurried back indoors, her face flushed with the cold. Since Bob's leg injury, she'd been more active, and it was doing her good.

She knocked into the magazines as she went to put the kettle on. She was reminded she'd meant to speak to Bob. He was in the spare bedroom, which they were using as a study. Bob had installed their computer there and put up some bookshelves. He was sitting reading a fishing journal, but looked at her over his reading glasses with a smile.

'You should have let me shovel that snow away.'

'I quite enjoyed the exercise. Anyway, you mustn't make your leg worse.'

'It's almost healed. I'll be able to dance with you on Christmas Day.'

'What nonsense!' Martha nudged him, laughing. 'We can hardly dance at a restaurant.'

'Are we still doing that, then?' Bob said, pushing his glasses up onto the bridge of his nose. 'I quite liked Kirsty's suggestion of inviting Simon's lot over.'

'We don't know them, though, do we? I'm not sure I want to spend Christmas Day with strangers.'

'Simon's hardly a stranger,' Bob said. 'I've played golf with him and we've done a bit of fishing together.'

'True, but what about his two nephews? We've never met them, and there's a child too.'

'I wouldn't mind, to be honest.' Bob sat up straight and set his journal down. 'A busy Christmas might be just what we need to distract us.'

'I'll think about it. Right now, I want to ask you about holidays.'

'What kind of holidays?' Bob asked, sounding wary.

'You know, the kind where you pack your bags and go somewhere and have fun,' she said brightly.

'Haven't we had this conversation? I don't want to plan a trip anywhere right now. There's Christmas coming up very fast, for a start. After that, I've got so many projects I want to get going on. I don't have time for a holiday, and I don't want one.'

'What about the magazines? You had the pages open at the cruises.'

'Oh . . . those.' Bob sighed. 'I know you'd like to travel. I was going to suggest that you speak to Frank and Babs about a short cruise.'

'I'm confused. You want me to organise us going on a cruise with our friends, but you don't want a holiday. Which is it?'

Bob pushed up out of the armchair and put his arms out to her. 'I meant for you to go with them on a week's cruise, not me.'

Martha took a swift breath. She pushed his arms away from her, appalled to discover there were tears welling in her eyes. 'I don't understand you. In fact, I'm beginning to think I don't really know you at all. How could you suggest such a thing?'

She turned blindly and went out of the room, ignoring Bob's pleading voice. In their bedroom, she shut the door and sat heavily on the bed. She heard his footsteps hesitate outside, then when she didn't answer him, they moved slowly away. Martha had never felt so alone in her whole life.

⋆ ⋆ ⋆

'I don't want to go to New York for Christmas,' William said.

He and Lara were in the classroom at the end of the day. The bell had rung and the pupils had gone, leaving a few pencil cases, lunch boxes and one coat in the room. There was a smell of glue sticks and a generous sprinkling of sparkles on the carpet. Another successful day in primary one.

'I didn't know you were going there,' Lara said. Stupid of her to feel a sense of loss. Of course Ian and William were free to spend Christmas anywhere they chose. But why somewhere so exotic?

'Do you mean York, rather than New York?' she tried.

'It's New York. Uncle Alan showed

me on a map. It's a long way. You have to go in an aeroplane.'

'Aren't you excited?'

'I was at first. I told Uncle Alan I really wanted to go. But then Dad told me Great Uncle Simon's coming home, and I don't want to miss him. Also, Uncle Alan's friend Karen is going to be in New York. I don't like her much.'

'Perhaps you'll enjoy it when you get there.'

'No, I won't. But I don't want to tell Uncle Alan. He'll be sad.'

'I see what you mean. Maybe you could tell your dad?'

'He'll be upset too. I know he will. He says he needs a holiday.'

'Tell you what — why don't I treat you to a hot chocolate in my favourite café, and we can talk about it some more?' She was keeping William for a few hours after school before dropping him home.

William brightened. He quickly put on his coat and got his school bag. He looked so hopeful that Lara's heart sank. He believed she'd be able to fix his problem, when the reality was she didn't have a clue. His hand slipped into hers, and his trusting face beamed up at her. Lara smiled back. Somehow she'd help him.

11

To say that the shopping mall was busy was an understatement. Kirsty searched for a word and came up with *frenzied*. She was crazy to be here. The noise level was set to explode eardrums, and she'd lost count of the number of times someone had bumped into her. Still, it was very festive, and a good place to lose the thoughts circling in her head. Those pesky thoughts involving her blue-eyed cowboy, Alan Carter. She was in love with Alan! There was wonder in those words. They made her heart sing. At the same time, they made her spirits swoop downwards, because it seemed it was all one way.

To be fair, it wasn't just Alan on her mind. Her mother was acting weirdly. Kirsty ought to be in her own shop right now, selling frantically to desperate Christmas shoppers. Instead, she'd had a late-evening call from Martha, asking if she could mind the shop that day. When Kirsty asked her why, she was told it was none of her business and to give a simple yes or no.

So here she was, footloose and fancy free as the saying went. She had her handbag on one shoulder and a couple of shopping bags in one hand. She'd spent a few hours hunting for presents, and had also bought a really gorgeous top she decided she'd wear on Christmas Day.

She glanced about for a café. There was plenty of choice. The problem was, most of them were full. The lunch hour was approaching and everyone had had the same idea. She noticed there were a couple of empty tables at one place and stepped smartly into the queue.

Standing there, musing on whether she'd have a cheese and tomato panini or a BLT, she was surprised when someone tapped her on the shoulder.

'Hi — you're Kirsty Perfect, aren't you?'

She looked at the woman without recognition. She was about the same age as Kirsty, with long blonde hair and a small baby in a carrier strapped to her chest. She wore trendy fringed jeans and a red velvet shirt that Kirsty immediately coveted.

'It's Bella Lomond. We were at school together?' She lilted the sentence so that it sounded like a question. Or maybe she wasn't sure she'd got it right. Her smile had faltered.

A vision of Bella Lomond arrived inside Kirsty's head. She'd looked rather different at school. Her hair had been a mousy brown and she'd had a mouthful of metal braces. Kirsty noticed this Bella had beautiful, even white teeth. So the braces had worked, then. Not to mention what a good-quality hair colour could do.

'Bella, hi. It's good to see you.'

'It's Bella Smith now.' She indicated her baby with a beaming smile. 'I got married last year.'

'Congratulations.' Kirsty said, forcing

a smile. She hated herself for the rush of jealousy that hit her.

'And now we've got baby Louie. Joe — that's my husband — he's so besotted with the little one. We're so happy . . . '

Kirsty let the other woman's words scatter over her like petals in a breeze. Did she really have to rub her happiness in so blatantly?

'So, are you married? Got kids?' Bella smiled, jiggling the baby carrier gently while the baby slumbered.

'No.' It came out sounding abrupt. Kirsty added a smile to soften it. 'I've got my own business and I love working for myself. I'm so busy.'

'That's great.'

They both knew she didn't mean it. Just as Kirsty began to think she was going to have to offer to share a table and have lunch with this stranger, the baby woke up. He began to whimper, and Bella's jiggling speeded up. The baby opened his tiny pink mouth and howled.

'He's hungry. I'm going to have go and feed him. Great to see you . . . we must catch up sometime.'

'Yes, we must.' No way on earth. 'Do you want some help?'

'No, I can manage. I'm used to it now.' Bella struggled away with her furious baby and her bags. The baby's crying gradually faded into the distance, swallowed up by all the other consumer noise.

Maybe she should be happy to be single, Kirsty mused as she picked up a BLT and a raspberry squash. She couldn't imagine looking after a baby. So why did she feel so low as she sat at her small table, alone, for lunch? Was it wrong to want to find love and a partner? And yes, at some point have a family. Whenever she flicked through magazines, they all screamed at her that the modern woman was happily single, highly successful and running her own business. She didn't need a man to be complete.

Kirsty didn't need a man to be

complete, either. She had her own business. She wasn't highly successful, but she made a comfortable income. It was just . . . it would be nice to have someone in her life whom she loved and who loved her. She hoped that made her a romantic rather than just needy.

She made another round of the queue for a latte and was lucky enough to find the same table unoccupied. Sitting there, her bags resting against her leg, sipping her latte and watching all the shoppers hurrying past, life was okay. She could forget Bella Lomond, now Smith, and her wonderful husband and child. She could be Kirsty Perfect, who often felt imperfect. She let it all wash over her with a sigh.

'Kirsty. There you are.' Alan's grin was wide as he sat down at her table.

'What a coincidence,' Kirsty said. 'Are you doing your Christmas shopping too?'

'The gallery was quiet, so I decided to close and come up to town. Looking around here, I can see where everyone has got to!'

'You didn't happen to see my mother, did you? She's running my shop today.'

Alan looked sheepish. 'Actually, I did step into your shop to see where you were. There was a stern-looking older lady behind the counter. So that's your mum, is it?'

'She isn't usually stern, to be honest. But she practically bullied me into allowing her to take over. I made myself scarce.'

'So where is he?' Alan glanced about as if expecting to see someone.

Kirsty was still processing the fact that it wasn't a coincidence that Alan had turned up at the mall. He'd asked her mother where she was.

'Where's who?' she said, puzzled.

'Your latest date. I assume that's why you're here. Some romantic Christmas shopping together, that sort of thing.'

Kirsty spoke slowly. 'Wait a minute. Let's get this straight. You thought I was meeting a date here at the mall. And yet you came here to see me? Does that make any sense?'

Alan blushed. If Kirsty had been in a better mood, she might have appreciated the way it contrasted with his piercing blue eyes and blond hair. As it was, she was on a low simmer of annoyance. How dare he! How dare he meddle in her affairs like that.

'Look, Kirsty, I'm sorry. I admit it — I worry about you meeting guys online. I thought . . . I thought I'd come along and keep an eye on you.'

Kirsty stood up so suddenly that her bags spilled at her feet. 'You came to spy on me!'

Alan stood up too. 'No, no, not like that. I'm your friend . . . '

'Some friend,' Kirsty cut in furiously. 'More like some kind of a creep, following me about 'for my own good.'' She swiped at the stuff that had fallen out of her bags and shoved it back in. Then, shoulders heaving with anger, she faced him. 'For your information,

I'm no longer dating. I've cancelled my subscription.'

Then she brushed past him and stomped away down the central hall, never minding who was in her way. Most people veered to let her go past. It was an amazingly effective way to get from point A to point B. Kirsty wished she'd bulldozed her way through the crowds earlier. Boy, was she simmering now. Alan Carter could go and . . . and . . . Oh! Bother it. Her shoulders lowered and her breathing calmed.

Kirsty stopped in an out-of-the-way corner. The shop next to her sold pretty candles and scents, and calming mystical music wafted out of its entrance. She allowed the atmosphere to seep into her. She wasn't very proud of herself. She'd called Alan a creep, but he was only concerned for her welfare. He shouldn't have been following her, though; she was a grown-up woman who could handle herself. Yet hadn't Martha and Lara voiced similar concerns? She ought to be flattered that he cared enough to watch out for her.

It was like a game of ping-pong in her head. One minute she was angry and indignant with him, the next she was ashamed of her behaviour. She knew he was a good, kind person. He only had her best interests at heart.

She made up her mind she'd go back and apologise. But when she got to the table, Alan had gone.

⋆　⋆　⋆

Alan knew he'd made a mistake. He shouldn't have gone to the mall. Instead of looking out for Kirsty, he'd made her angry. Somehow he couldn't keep away from her. He'd tried, he really had. Especially after the mistletoe. He'd been so close to kissing her. Her lips had been so very enticing, and he'd been certain she wouldn't push him away. There had been a magical moment between them.

But it was wrong. He wasn't ready for another relationship so soon after

Karen. It wasn't fair on Kirsty. He didn't know what he had to offer. Or what his feelings were.

After she stormed off, he wasn't sure what to do. He was delighted to hear she wasn't dating anymore. At least not online dating. She was so attractive, he was sure she'd find someone soon. And good luck to her, he thought, nodding decisively. Yes, indeed. He hoped she'd find a guy who loved her, if that was what she was searching for.

Finding he was getting some strange looks, he decided he'd join the queue. He might as well get a coffee. There was no point going after Kirsty. The queue had lengthened, and it took ages for him to get back round to where he had his coffee and was searching for a table.

He stopped. Kirsty was sitting at a table, watching him. She smiled slightly as he caught sight of her. Alan's chest tightened. He walked over.

'May I join you?' he said politely, as if they hadn't parted on an argument.

'I'd love it if you did,' she said in

return, clearing a space for him by putting her bag down. 'Look, I'm sorry for how I spoke to you earlier. I was out of order.'

'No, I was out of order,' he countered. 'I shouldn't have come here. You were right. It's your life and you don't need me looking out for you.'

'I was too harsh. It was a kind thought.'

'You've given up on the dating site?'

'It wasn't working out.'

He didn't ask her for further details. She didn't look as if she'd volunteer any. Her shapely mouth was set.

'My Christmas plans have taken another turn,' he said, changing the subject.

'In a good way or not?'

He was glad to see her good humour restored. She tucked a lock of her dark hair behind an ear and leaned towards him to hear his answer. He liked that about her. She had a knack of focusing on a person as if nothing else mattered. As if it was just them in the whole mall.

'It's hard to say. You know we were invited to New York by Karen. Then I heard from the hospital that Uncle Simon is coming home before the twenty-fifth. William was set on the adventure, and Ian told me he was looking forward to a holiday. So then I didn't feel I could say no to New York.'

'But what were you to do about Simon?' Kirsty finished for him.

'Exactly. Then William came home from school the day before yesterday and said he had something to say to me. He looked like he was bursting with it. He said he didn't want to go to New York after all.'

'Did he say why?'

'He doesn't want to miss seeing Uncle Simon.'

'That's great, then. It's all sorted.'

'Mmm, not quite,' Alan said, turning the coffee cup around on the table.

'You mean Karen will be upset?'

'I doubt Karen will be perturbed in the slightest,' Alan said drily. 'She's got other options, I'm sure. No, I'm worried about Ian. My brother was looking forward to a holiday. Instead, he's going to find himself in Uncle Simon's house over the holidays. He's talking about moving out with William into a rented flat. I feel I've let him down.'

'It's one of those situations where you can't please everyone,' Kirsty said. 'I have a proposition to make.'

'I'm all ears.'

'How would you like to come to ours for Christmas? You, Ian, William, and Simon too. My parents would love it.'

'We couldn't possibly . . . '

'Alan, don't dismiss it out of hand. Please think about it. I'm serious. We're looking for a different kind of Christmas this year too.'

'But you couldn't possibly want a bunch of strangers turning up to celebrate with you.'

'You're not strangers. How can you say that? You and I know each other, and Lara and Ian seem to be spending quite a bit of time together. My Dad knows Simon. My Mum isn't generally stern; she's usually the life and soul of any party. To be honest, you'd be doing us a favour by accepting. Otherwise, I'm not sure I'll be looking forward to Christmas this year at all. And that, coming from a massive Christmas fan such as I am, is pretty awful.'

Secretly, Alan was pleased at the thought of spending the festive day with Kirsty. He never tired of looking at her. He liked the way she was so easy to read. Her mobile face showed her bright quicksilver emotions, and he felt she always said what she thought, straight down the line. Quite unlike Karen, he reflected, who he'd never really understood; she so often said one thing but acted quite differently.

'Well, if you're sure your parents really won't mind?'

'They'll be delighted,' Kirsty said firmly.

She grabbed his hands impulsively, eyes shiny as she described her plans for the holidays. Alan heard some of it, but his concentration zoomed right in to the feel of her warm, smooth skin and the gentle pressure of her nails on his fingers. It was as if the whole world had focused right down to this single sensation. He skipped a breath and then had to draw an extra-deep one into his lungs.

Slowly, he pulled his hands free. Kirsty didn't seem to notice. She simply then used her hands to gesticulate excitedly as she chatted. Alan swallowed. He couldn't ignore it. Whatever his feelings towards Kirsty, he couldn't deny that he was extremely attracted to her physically. He had to try to hide it. He didn't want another relationship so soon after Karen. Which meant that all he had to offer Kirsty was his friendship. Some friend he'd turn out to be if she knew he wanted her. That wasn't fair on her. No, it had to be just friends. He could do that, right?

'Why are you nodding to yourself?'

Kirsty asked, amusement colouring her voice.

'Sorry, was I? Just . . . just looking forward to Christmas,' he said lamely.

'Me too, now that you're all coming to visit,' she said with a grin.

★　★　★

Back in the shop, Martha was finding it difficult to keep a cheerful smile on her face for the endless customers. If one more person asked for a box of crackers, she'd scream. She kept having to go through to the back storeroom for more. In an unusual five minutes where no one was in the shop, she quickly tidied her hair and popped the kettle on. She was exhausted.

Still, being in the shop was a distraction from the tense atmosphere at home. Since their argument, she and Bob had been distant and polite with each other. That was two whole days of a chilled and pointed silence. It wasn't as if they could get away from each other, either, since they were retired and Bob's leg meant he didn't go out much. There was no working day apart that might have allowed them to mull it over and forgive in peace.

Which was why Martha had demanded Kirsty give her the shop for a day. Otherwise she might have gone completely mad. Now, in the back room with a hot cup of tea and hopefully no interruptions for a few minutes, she did think about it all.

She was very hurt that Bob wanted her to go on holiday without him. Did he want a break from her? Did he want rid of her? Putting her cup down with a sigh, Martha shook her head. She did know him better than that. They'd been married so long, she knew him better than he knew himself. She shouldn't have reacted so badly.

Bob knew she wanted to go on a cruise, and he didn't. He was content to be at home with his various projects. He was trying to find a way of making them both happy. She saw that now.

But it still stung.

Martha knew she had to apologise. She had to make it up with him. They had never had an argument which ran on for days. It was her fault for being so sensitive. The trouble was, she did want a holiday. Not with Babs and Frank, though. She wanted a holiday with Bob.

12

It was exactly one week until Christmas Day, and it was a dull grey and drizzly Saturday. Lara had got up early and dressed warmly. She packed her wellingtons, a hat and gloves and a flask of hot peppermint tea into the boot of her car. She had promised William that she'd take him to the beach to collect pebbles for his school project. There were only a couple of days of school left, and they were going to make festive paperweights. Knowing some of her pupils would forget to bring stones, Lara decided she'd gather some herself for the Monday.

To her delight, when she went to pick up William, Ian had asked if he could come to the beach too. He'd been working too hard and had to get out of the house or he'd be back at his desk, he told her. Lara drove them to the coast and parked up in the empty car park.

They sat for a moment, cocooned inside the car. There was a teasing breeze that buffeted them. Outside, the world was grey. Lara usually loved the view from the car park. She could look across the rocky beach to the sea and the hills and towns on the other side of the estuary and then the wide and endless sky. But today, it all looked rather grim.

The rocky beach was so dark the stones looked almost black and the seaweed greasy yellow. The sea was a wide strip of dull pewter. The hills on the far side were greyish-brown and streaked with some leftover snow, and the towns were hardly visible apart from one or two orange lights. The day was dim, as if the world couldn't bother to drag itself to daylight.

Lara shivered.

'You cold?' Ian asked. He took off his scarf and laid it round her shoulders.

She smiled. 'Thanks. I was just

getting cold feet, that's all. It looks horrible and gloomy out there.'

'I've got cold feet too, but I actually mean they *are* cold,' Ian laughed, kicking his boots together. 'If we don't get walking, I think I'll freeze up entirely.'

'You won't really, will you, Dad?' William asked, attempting to squeeze his body through between the two front seats.

'I'm only joking, son,' Ian reassured him. 'What do you think? Are you ready for a brisk walk along the beach?'

'I have to get some good pebbles,' William said, 'don't I, Lara?'

'That's right. We'll get some really good ones on this beach, I promise. Okay, I'm being a coward by sitting here. Shall we get going?'

'Let's count down from ten,' William suggested.

They began to chant the numbers slowly and loudly. Lara thought if anyone was watching them, they'd wonder if they were all out of their minds. Then as they shouted zero, they all flung open their car doors into the breeze and jumped out.

Lara found herself laughing into the wind. The air was cold on her teeth and her cheeks tingled with the frostiness. Yet she was filled with the utmost happiness to be here, at the gloomy, downright ugly beach, because she was with two of her favourite people.

'It's not usually so drab,' she said, seeing Ian's doubtful face cast seawards. 'Honestly, I love coming here in the summer. You can look for fish in the rock pools and even paddle in the sea. There's lots of gorse in flower, and it smells like coconut. It's heavenly. Kirsty and I have very fond memories of this beach. We used to come here with Mum and Dad when we were small and have lovely family picnics.'

'I'd like to do that,' William said, tugging on Ian's hand. 'Can we do that, Dad? Can we have a picnic with Lara here?'

Ian turned up his collar with his free

hand. 'I think we'll wait until summer for that, old chap. But if we're still here by then, I'd love to.'

'Are you thinking of moving elsewhere?' Lara asked, her stomach lurching.

'I haven't decided yet. We'll have to move out of Simon's house after Christmas. He's coming home, and he won't want us cluttering the place up.'

'But you could buy a place in town.' It was none of her business, Lara thought, but she suddenly couldn't bear the thought of losing them. It was strange how quickly she'd become close to both Ian and William.

'Yes, I could buy a house here. I don't know. I want to enjoy the holidays first and get a couple of big projects out of the way before I make any serious decisions.'

'Of course,' Lara said. She concentrated on getting her wellingtons on and tried not to imagine them leaving town. She jammed her hat on her head, slipped on her gloves and led the way down the narrow path to the beach.

The rocks and stones were slippery with the stranded seaweed and a covering of thin frost. It glittered but failed to brighten the beach up. Instead, Lara had to move very carefully from rock to rock to prevent falling. Ian took her hand, and together they moved across to a less rocky section where there were plenty of rounded pebbles.

William had no problem getting across the surfaces. He had the natural buoyancy of youth and none of the caution needed by his elders. He rapidly found several amazing smooth pebbles and held them up for Lara's approval. 'This is the best — look, Lara. Or is this one better?' He frowned and crouched down on the grit to find some more.

'I need to get a handful, too,' Lara said to Ian. 'Most kids will bring a stone, but there will probably be a few who won't. I want every child to make a paperweight. It's about the only lesson they'll get before the show.'

'I'm guessing it's an art lesson,' Ian teased as they wandered across towards the sea. The tide was far out.

'Yes, it's art, but it's also going to be maths and English.'

'Maths?'

'A lesson in how to weigh and measure their pebbles.'

'And English?'

'They can write about their stones, maybe put them as characters into a story.'

'That's clever,' Ian said, picking up a few pebbles and showing them to her.

Lara picked the best ones and threw the others into the sea. Ian glanced back to make sure William was okay. Lara did too. The little boy was in a world of his own. He was still crouched amongst the pebbles and stones, a pile of them in a small cairn beside him. He'd found a stick and was drawing in the grit. It wasn't sand. Sand was fine and golden. But it was enough to draw lines in.

'It's not clever,' Lara grinned, picking

up the thread of their conversation again as they wandered about. 'It's called being a teacher. Everything can be a lesson if you try and use your imagination.'

'William is certainly thriving in your class. Thank you. He's a different boy from when we left our old home.'

'He's made some lovely friends, and that helps. He's clever and inquisitive, so he's doing very well. He . . . ' Lara hesitated; she didn't want to upset Ian. 'He . . . must miss his mother.'

'He misses the idea of a mother.' Ian stared out to sea, then looked to Lara. 'He never knew his mum, sadly. She died shortly after he was born. She had cancer and she knew she was going. Being Alicia, she left everything in order for her boys, as she called us. She left lists and instructions. She wanted us to be able to be happy without her.'

'She sounds lovely.'

'She was lovely. In every way. She'd have been a wonderful mother, but she ran out of time.'

Lara wasn't sure what to say. It was so sad. Ian clearly loved his wife, and William had a gap in his young life that couldn't be filled. Ian surprised her by picking up a flat stone and skimming it across the surface of the water.

'Bet you can't do that,' he challenged.

He didn't want to dwell on his sadness; Lara understood that. Even though Alicia had been gone for five years, it was still painful. So she quickly found a flattish pebble and sent it skimming into the water. It bounced for five, one more than Ian's attempt.

'Hey, you didn't tell me you were a champion skimmer,' he joked.

'There's lots of things about me you don't know,' Lara laughed.

'I'd like to find out,' he murmured.

For a moment, their gazes caught above the stones and currents and the edge of the sluggish sea. The mournful hoot of a boat's horn made them both jump and chuckle, and the moment was forgotten. The skimming contest ended in a draw. Lara felt quite warm with the effort and took off her hat, letting her long golden hair stream out, whipping her face. She felt the comforting softness of Ian's scarf around her neck. Beside her, Ian's tall figure was swathed in a long woollen navy coat. His face was red from the cold and exertion, and his eyes twinkled in glee as he aimed stone throws at a floating log going past.

What they were doing was a childish game and simply pleasurable. It didn't matter that the day was dark and brooding or that the wind was slicingly cold. There was fun to be had here. It was nice to be away from the town for a little while. She had homework and housework to be done. But it could all wait.

Then she remembered Mark. She needed to know what had happened. It was a pity to bring up the subject when they were having fun, but she had to hear it from Ian. 'What did Mark have to say the other day?' she asked.

Ian threw a final stone before answering. It hit the log with a dull thud. Neither of them cheered. A current took the log further out into the estuary, sliding it along on its journey out to sea. 'He agreed to stop harassing you, as I said.'

Ian had texted her that same morning. She'd picked up his message at break time and been very relieved by it, but also curious as to how he'd managed to get Mark to agree.

'I'm surprised he was so reasonable,' she pressed gently.

'He was, in the end.'

'I knew it had to be more than a quick conversation with him. I'd like to know what happened.'

'Is there any point going over it?' Ian said. 'He says he won't bother you anymore, and that's the main thing.'

Lara paused. Her boots were covered with grey grit and wet mud. She'd have to wash them off when she got home. Then she was annoyed with herself for dodging Ian's question. It was her flaw.

She always backed down from any unpleasantness. And look where that had got her in the past. At Mark's beck and call, that was where. She'd spent two years tiptoeing around his dark emotions, trying to make sure he didn't get angry, even when it meant putting her own interests last.

Well, she thought, she wasn't going to do that anymore. She was busy building a new life, one that most definitely did not include her ex-fiancé. In fact, she was ashamed that she'd let him hang around her the way he had. She should have told him a plain and bold *no*. No, she wasn't going to go for a drink with him. No, it was not all right for him to wait at the school gates each day for her. No, she was never going back to him.

Lara felt a surge of unusual confidence. Perhaps it was having Ian's tall figure right next to her, or perhaps it was the invigorating breeze and harsh surroundings of the winter beach. Whatever it was, she knew deep inside that she'd changed. She had her own flat; she had a good, secure job that she loved; she had a wonderful family who loved her. She had a good life. All she needed was to believe in herself.

'I do want to know what happened,' she said firmly. 'Please tell me. And don't leave anything out. I'm not going to be scared anymore by Mark.'

'Okay,' Ian said, 'that's the attitude. I'll tell you what I said and his response. He backed down and promised to leave you alone after I threatened to tell the police about the damage to your car. He was worried he'd lose his job.'

'If he does any more damage to my property, I *will* go to the police,' Lara said. 'I'm sorry, Ian. You were right — I should have gone and filed a complaint that morning. I just didn't want to make it official. But I see now I was wrong.'

Ian put his arm around her. It seemed like the most natural gesture; and when he pulled her close and hugged her, Lara felt her heart would burst from her chest with happiness.

'Well done,' he whispered into her hair. 'You're so brave and strong.'

'Me? I hardly think so. I'm a wimp,' she murmured into his coat as it brushed her face.

He smelt of damp wool, frosty air and soap. It was a heady mixture, and she wanted to burrow in and stay there forever. She didn't move while Ian described his encounter with Mark. Then she opened her eyes to see William's curious gaze on them. Quickly she pulled away from Ian.

'Look at this one,' William said, holding up a triangular stone.

Then the heavens opened up and sheets of icy rain water poured down on them. Lara screamed and they all ran as fast as possible back to the car. Although fast wasn't really an option, as the stones were so slippery. Picking their way gingerly around the seaweed and finally up the path to the car park, they were all totally drenched. Lara unlocked the car and they dived inside.

They stared at each other in horror. Lara was aware of freezing cold water pouring down her back and the fact that her jeans were completely sodden. Her legs were so, so cold and wet. Her socks were soaked too inside her wellingtons. Her hands were an odd shade of purple when she took off her gloves and wrung them out.

She looked over at Ian. His hair was flattened to his head and rain droplets trickled down his face. His coat was black with the amount of water held in the wool. She craned her neck to see William in the back seat. He was like a small merman, his clothes plastered to him and not an inch of him dry. He wore a huge smile as if they'd had an adventure.

Ian burst out laughing. 'What a bunch of scarecrows we are.'

'I'll put the car heater on,' Lara said, starting up the engine.

A moment later, warm air blasted from the vents, but it wasn't going to be enough. 'Why don't we stop in at my parents' house?' she suggested. 'It's closest to the beach and we can get dried out there. Otherwise, we'll catch a chill. I don't want to get my cold again or have you two ill over Christmas because I invited you out here today.'

'Sounds like a good idea.' Ian wiped rainwater away from his forehead with an equally wet coat cuff. 'Your parents won't mind?'

'Not at all. They'll be delighted to get visitors. Mum loves a bit of drama, and quite honestly I think she needs some these days. She's bored in her new house.'

Soon they were drawing up in front of the modern bungalow, and parked on the street outside.

'This is a recent development, then?' Ian said. 'It's very nicely laid out, and the houses are good quality.'

'Tell that to my mum,' Lara said with a smile. 'She's still not sure it was a good thing moving here.'

The rain had stopped and a weak,

watery sun blinked between the black clouds. Another downpour threatened and they hurried to the door. Lara only pressed the doorbell once before Martha appeared.

'You're like drowned rats! Come in, come in,' she said, standing back to give them space. 'Don't worry about the drips, just leave your boots in the hall and I'll get some towels.'

'Mum, this is Ian and his son William,' Lara said quickly. 'William's in my class, and Ian's . . . '

'Simon's nephew. Yes dear, I know. It's lovely to meet you both.'

'I do apologise, Mrs Perfect, for our appearance. We were on the beach when the downpour caught us out.'

Lara saw the interested gleam in her mother's eyes as she glanced between Lara and Ian. She'd have to nip that idea in the bud. There was no romance going on.

'Towels, Mum?'

'Oh yes, of course, darling. Why don't you show Ian and William where the bathroom is and I'll get some.'

Soon they were all dried out and sitting in the small but neat living room where the fire was on, and the air deliciously cosy. Ian was wearing some of Bob's clothes, and Martha had found some clothes for William. The trouser hems and sweatshirt sleeves were rolled up many times over, but at least he was dressed. Lara recognised the jeans and top as old clothes from Kirsty's teenage years, no doubt destined for a charity shop but never sent. Her mother was quite sentimental about her children, keeping many mementoes of their growing up. Lara kept extra clothes here in a wardrobe in the spare room, so had no trouble finding a clean, dry pair of jeans and a jersey to put on.

Bob offered a plate of biscuits around. Martha set out mugs and poured hot chocolate.

'You have a very nice house,' Ian said, settling back onto the sofa beside Lara. His shoulder pressed slightly against hers but she didn't move. She was acutely aware of his long leg just next to hers.

'Ian's an architect,' Lara added.

'We're growing to like it,' Martha said. 'It was strange at first, adjusting to smaller rooms and no staircases. I like the garden best. It's a pity it's such a horrible day or I'd show you outside.'

Ian got up and walked over to the window. He was silent for a minute. Then he turned to them. 'Have you considered putting in a conservatory? You've got the space to do it, at the back here. Then you could enjoy your garden all year round.'

Lara saw her mother perk up immediately. Bob, too, looked interested.

'I like that idea,' Martha said, looking at her husband. 'Bob, what you do think?'

Was it Lara's imagination, or did her father seem particularly keen to please her mother? That generally meant they'd had words and he needed to make amends. She hoped it wasn't about Hambly again. They really had to move on.

'Keep talking,' Bob said to Ian.

Lara listened while Ian scoped out possible designs. She saw the enthusiasm he had for creating living space, and his energy was infectious. Bob and Martha were just as caught up in the idea as he was.

*   *   *

When their visitors had gone, Martha was buzzing with excitement. Ian's plans, sketched on paper, lay on the coffee table in the living room. Bob was looking at them, deep in thought. She went and sat beside him, taking his hand and squeezing it gently.

They had made up from their disagreement about the cruise. Martha had apologised for her behaviour and so had Bob. He'd only wanted the best for her, he'd said. Martha said she realised that. They left it there, almost sorted but with a few doubtful threads hanging. Martha didn't think he really understood her need for a holiday, while Bob, in turn, couldn't understand why she'd been so upset with him.

'Well?' she said. 'Shall we?'

'Put in a conservatory? I can't decide right away. It needs a lot of thought.' He got a pencil and scribbled some notes and drew some arrows on Ian's sketch.

'Oh, let's not wait ten years to do it,' Martha said. 'Let's be spontaneous and go for it.' She wanted to laugh at the way Bob's eyebrows rose towards the ceiling. 'Seriously, dear. I want this.'

'I thought you wanted a holiday. You do realise if we do this, we won't have the cash for a holiday for a year or two.'

'Mmm, that is true,' Martha said. 'However, I want this more. Think how wonderful it would be to be sitting right now in a conservatory with gorgeous house plants surrounding us and the garden on view three quarters of the way round. That's the way Ian said it'll be. Not only that, but it will be a project for both of us to work on. It'll be nice spending time together with a hobby in common.'

'Do you think Lara and Ian . . . ?'

'I think we shouldn't ask. Just keep our fingers crossed.'

Bob put his arm around her. 'If we do get a conservatory, I think we might be able to put a little money aside for a weekend at a country hotel. Would you like that?'

Martha's answer was to kiss her surprised husband full on the lips.

13

'This is extraordinary. I absolutely love it.'

The woman speaking with such enthusiasm was a regular at the gallery and often bought pieces of art. Now she held up the picture in its gilt frame as if it was a rare treasure.

'It's very good,' Alan agreed, accepting it from her and wrapping it securely in bubble wrap and brown paper. He tied the string with a flourish. He was getting used to all the everyday practices in the gallery.

'Is she a local artist?'

'Yes, she is.' Alan decided not to say that the artist in question worked in the shop next door. 'She's sold a couple of paintings through this gallery previously. Before my time, though.'

'Oh, what a pity I missed them. You will give me prior warning on the next one, won't you?'

She slid her business card into Alan's hand with a secretive wink. Alan knew from Simon's customer files that she often snapped up pieces on private preview before they even made it onto the gallery walls. He was thrilled for Kirsty that her painting had sold, and to someone so passionate about art. He decided he'd go round and tell her in person at lunch when he could safely shut the gallery.

She had barely disappeared with her new purchase when Alan's mobile rang. It was the hospital. Mr Timmons was ready to go home, and could someone please collect him? It looked as if Alan would be shutting the gallery well before lunch after all. Still, the sale of Kirsty's painting meant that he didn't need to worry if nothing else was bought or reserved that day.

He had to wait a half hour at the hospital while Simon's medicines were prepared. The old man looked frail but glad to be getting out and going home.

Alan managed to get a wheelchair and take his uncle down in the lift to the car. It was a busy place, and he wondered if the hospital was being emptied as much as possible for the Christmas holidays.

'You're looking much better,' he said as he clipped Simon's seat belt into its lock.

'Feeling it too,' Simon said. 'I can't wait to get home.'

But when he finally got Simon and his hospital bags over the threshold, the old man looked about with mounting annoyance. 'Where's all my stuff? What have you done with my books? And where's my round table gone?'

'Sorry,' Alan said hastily. 'We rearranged the living room and kitchen somewhat. Don't worry, it can all be put back just as you like it. We needed a bit of extra space, as Ian and William are staying here too.'

'Are they? You didn't tell me that.'

'I did ask you if they could come and stay and you said yes. You said you were happy your home was being looked after so well.'

'I did? Must have slipped my memory. Where's the boy?'

'He's at school. Last couple of days before the holidays. And Ian's out at a work meeting. He'll be back for dinner and said to tell you he's looking forward to seeing you.'

Simon made a harrumphing sound. Alan reckoned he was embarrassed he'd forgotten he'd said they could all stay here. It was clear he didn't approve of all their tidying-up efforts either. Thank goodness Alan had stopped Karen's excessive cleaning suggestions!

'I'll have a seat on the sofa while you make tea. Then I want to hear all about my gallery.'

'Good idea. I'll tell you about the plans for Christmas too.'

'You can tell me them right now. What plans? I wasn't going to bother with Christmas this year. I'm too tired.'

'We've been invited to Bob and Martha Perfect's home for Christmas

Day. But if it's too much for you, we can cancel.'

There was a silence during which Simon chewed on his teeth and made various sniffing noises. Alan tactfully left him on the sofa and retreated to the kitchen to make a brew. He took his first deep breath since arriving at the hospital. This was harder than he'd thought it would be. He understood it was difficult for Simon, coming home to find it taken over by his nephews, and nothing quite as it should be. He'd have to be updated on how the gallery was going as well. There, surely, he would have nothing to complain about. Alan had devoted many hours of overtime to looking after the place.

He'd spoken to Lisa about the coffee shop, taking up Kirsty's suggestions of scoping out how to expand the space. She was willing to sell to Simon at a very reasonable rate as he was a neighbouring business and a friend. Alan had sketched ideas and Ian had run them up into a professional architectural mock-up plan showing how it could look. He even had some rough costs, ballpark figures for Simon to consider.

When he went back through to the living room, Simon looked calmer. 'I like Bob Perfect. He plays a mean round of golf. Assuming I'm feeling healthy, I'd like to go there for Christmas Day.'

'That's great. I'll let them know.'

'Now, more importantly, how's my gallery?'

'It's doing very well.' Alan told him how he was running it and how many pictures had been sold or promised. A well-known artist had been in touch to arrange a show there in the New Year. Simon grunted and Alan took this as approval. Perhaps now was the time to mention his big ideas for expansion.

'You want to do what? No, no, no. What are you thinking?' Simon almost slipped off the sofa in his agitation.

'It's only an idea, Uncle Simon. Please calm down. This can't be good for you, just out of hospital. We don't want you going back in.' Alan put his hand reassuringly on his uncle's arm. He felt the jump of muscles and wished he never mentioned his ideas.

'My gallery is fine just as it is.' Simon emphasised the word 'my'. 'After Christmas I'll be well enough to go back to running it. You must have a job to go to. When are you going back to work?'

He couldn't have been any clearer, Alan thoughtful ruefully. He wanted Alan out. Yes, Simon was thankful Alan had stepped in to look after the house and gallery; but naturally he wanted those back now without interference. Alan didn't blame him. It was time he picked up the reins of his own life. But he hadn't worked out yet what that life was to be.

'You're right, I do need to get back to my own things after the holidays. Ian's talking about buying a house too, so you'll have your own space back very soon.'

'Don't think I'm ungrateful, because I'm not. I can see you boys have looked after my place very well and stopped any potential burglaries. You've kept my gallery open when it might have been shut for weeks. I thank you for that. But you're young; I mustn't keep you back from forging your future.'

'Shall I tell Lisa you're not interested in buying her coffee shop, then? It's only fair she puts it back on the open market. She was doing us a favour by waiting for your answer.'

'Leave it to me. I'll talk to her. I'll miss Lisa next door. I don't like change.'

That was an understatement. Alan hid a smile. He was very fond of his uncle, but he could be hard work sometimes.

A while later, when Simon was upstairs for an afternoon nap and Alan was considering going back to the gallery, his phone rang again. He was sitting in his room, looking at his easel and an unfinished watercolour of a river and mountain. It was going to remain unfinished. He had a pile of paintings he'd played about with, and had finally admitted to himself that he was never going to be very good. He was much better at assessing other people's work and selling it.

When he answered his phone, it was his law firm. Despite what he'd said to Karen, he'd never got around to telling them he was leaving. He was still, as far as he knew, on a period of extended leave. He had been reluctant to cut that last tie with his career. His future was blurry and without definite shape. However, it looked as if its shape was about to be decided for him.

'Mr Winters wants to know if you're coming back,' the secretary said.

'I'm on leave until January.'

'That's all changed. There's a new client and the casework is going to be large. Mr Winters needs you back.' The secretary sounded efficient but completely disinterested in whether Alan did or did not come back. She was merely Mr Winters's communicator, her tone indicated.

What was he to say? Alan had half-hoped that Simon would ask him to stay on at the gallery. If it was extended, there was easily enough work for two of them in running it. He loved the gallery, but it was Simon's; and once he was back, there'd be no space for Alan. Could he buy his own shop to run as a gallery? A shot of adrenaline ran through him. It was a scary but exciting notion.

'Mr Carter? Are you there?'

'Sorry, I was thinking . . . ' Not about corporate law. Didn't that tell him something important? He wasn't interested in corporate law at all. If he was honest, he never had been. He'd studied law at university to please his parents. Then it had been a logical step to take it up as a career. He was good at it, but it never stirred him emotionally. It paid well and gave him a comfortable lifestyle, but that was all. It wasn't enough to feed his soul.

240

Alan knew that now.

'Mr Winter needs an answer,' the long-suffering secretary said. She allowed a hint of impatience to seep in to her professional telephone voice.

'Please tell Mr Winter that I'm handing in my notice. I'm not coming back. Email me the necessary paperwork and I'll make sure it's returned promptly. Goodbye.'

Alan ended the call with a mounting sense of excitement and trepidation. What had he done? He'd done the right thing. The essential thing. He was now free! It was a terrifying thought. He comforted himself with the thought that he had enough savings to keep him for a while until he found what he was looking for.

Then it struck him hard — if he couldn't work with Simon at his gallery, he was going to have to move away. There wasn't room in a small town for two art galleries. That meant leaving Ian and William. He'd got used to them being around and he liked being a hands-on uncle. Lurking behind that thought was another . . . he'd be leaving Kirsty too.

It shouldn't matter, he told himself. He tried to shut off his dismay by tidying up his paintbrushes and paints and stacking them on his bookshelf. He wouldn't need them again. He tore down his latest masterpiece and folded it up, then threw it in the bin. It was an ending. He couldn't paint. A door shut. He couldn't work in the gallery. Another door shut.

Impatiently, he headed downstairs. He'd go to Kirsty's shop and tell her about her painting. At least that was some good news.

Kirsty was busy with a froth of tissue paper, silky red ribbon and a delicate glass angel. She mouthed 'hello' and 'wait' at him while she dealt with her customer. Then he was alone with her. He took a moment to drink in the sight of her. She was wearing a spectacular festive jumper with a reindeer's face smiling on it, and she had an elf's cap on her glossy dark hair.

'Loving the look,' he said with a grin.

'Thanks. Less than a week to go,' she laughed. 'I'm counting down the days with my collection of Christmas clothing. Pop in tomorrow and see my Christmas pudding dress, complete with icing done in white lace and my fantastic felted holly leaves collar.'

'I can't wait. Listen, I've got some great news for you.'

She leaned on the counter, supporting her chin on her hands, eyes shiny with expectation.

'Your painting sold and the buyer was raving about it. She wants first dibs on your next one.'

Kirsty screamed and ran round the edge of the counter to hug him. Then she went up on tiptoe to kiss him. Going over it all in detail later, Alan realised she meant it to be a peck on his cheek. Unfortunately, just as she did so, he moved his head and their lips met. Without logical thought, he pulled her closer and pressed his mouth more deeply onto hers. She tasted sweet and fresh and warm.

Who was first to pull away? He replayed it over and over but couldn't decide. They sprang apart. Kirsty's fingers touched her lips. He still felt the impression of her mouth under his.

'Alan?' she whispered.

Her hand stretched out towards him. But Alan stepped back, cursing himself. What had he done? He'd walked, no he had run, across an invisible line. The line that straddled a friendship or a relationship. Horrified, he shook his head as she tried to speak.

'I'm sorry, I shouldn't have done that.'

'It's okay, Alan. It wasn't just you, it was me too. We both wanted that kiss. I . . . I want to tell you . . . I think I'm in love with you.'

'Kirsty — don't. Please. I can't do this. We're friends. That's all we can be. I like you very much, but I've barely split from Karen. I can't rush straight into another relationship, don't you see that? I don't want to hurt you. I don't know what I feel anymore . . . if I have any love to offer. You're very attractive, but . . . '

Now it was Alan's turn to put out his hand, seeking her understanding. But it was too late. Kirsty pushed him away and ran into the back room, slamming the door.

14

'It's not about *having* a conservatory, as such,' Martha said. 'Oh, I'm not explaining myself very well. What I'm trying to say is that it's as much about spending time with your father as it is about having a nice room to enjoy the garden from. Dad and I . . . well, there's a danger we could find ourselves living sort of separate lives. He's got his golf and fishing and DIY, and I've got . . . well, I'm not sure these days what I've got. I've lost touch with my old friends, and I gave up on my hobbies, so I need to find something to fill the gap.'

Lara waited while her mother got things off her chest. They were in Lara's school cupboard. Luckily it was a very large, airy cupboard. Primary One were away in the assembly hall with Moira Mellon, who was orchestrating one last run-through of the nativity. The local piano teacher had arrived and in the distance they could hear her belting through the carols and the children singing. The actual nativity was in the afternoon, with a winter festival following it. There was to be food and drink for the parents and carers and Primary Seven were to be the waiters. The whole school buzzed with barely suppressed excitement. Lara guessed there wasn't much studying going on that morning in any of the classes.

Meanwhile, in her school cupboard, they were supposed to be sorting through the remaining costumes and props for the afternoon. Martha had been drafted in as the seamstress and general helper, as she was every year.

'I think it's a great idea,' Lara said, holding up a large gold cloth for Martha's approval. 'Only, is there a danger you focus on the conservatory?'

'What do you mean?'

'Perhaps you should organise a lunch date with your old friends and see if you can invigorate the friendships again. As for hobbies, why don't you join a club in the New Year and make some new friends that way?'

'You're right, dear. I'll do that.'

'What about Dad and the holiday you wanted?' Lara folded the cloth and put it on the ever-increasing pile of items needed for the show.

'It's a bit like the conservatory. I worked out that it wasn't so much a holiday I needed as time spent with your father. The cruise was a way of being together. Now that I've realised that, I don't care if I ever go on a cruise. If I can be with Dad, sawing wood or poring over the conservatory plans, I'll be perfectly happy.'

'A weekend at a country hotel does sound marvellous, though.'

'Yes, it'll be very nice. But if we don't go, I won't be disappointed. Now, shall we take this great big bundle of stuff out into the classroom? I think I'll go crazy in your cupboard if I have to stay here another half hour.'

They put all the materials onto Lara's neat, clear desk and began to sort it into groups. There were capes and hats, angel wings from last year's show, and plastic food, amongst other things.

'I wanted to come round and tell you and Dad about Mark,' Lara said, 'but I've been so hectic I haven't had a moment.'

'What about Mark?' Martha's shoulders stiffened and her busy hands hovered over the materials.

'Nothing to worry about. In fact it's good news. He's stopped pestering me, and I think I've seen the back of him for good.'

'That's a relief. How did you manage that?'

'Ian had a few words with him.'

'How very good of him. He's a nice chap, isn't he?'

'Mum,' Lara warned, 'don't start getting ideas.'

'Oh, darling, you can't stay away from men for the rest of your life because of your experiences with Mark.'

'You're right, but maybe I'm not ready.'

'All I'm saying is, don't put up barriers. You'll know when you've found the right man. Talking of which, how's Kirsty? Has she been in touch? I haven't heard from her since she persuaded us to host Christmas for all and sundry.'

'You don't mind, do you?'

Martha laughed. 'Not at all. In fact, I'm looking forward to it very much. Dad and I have drawn up a huge food list, and I've made the cake and the puddings.'

'You'll be glad to hear, then, that Kirsty's given up on the online dating. She came round to see me last night.'

'I have to say I'm very relieved at that.'

'So am I, but there's something bothering her. She wouldn't tell me what was upsetting her, but for once she didn't mention Alan Carter, which made me wonder if they'd fallen out.'

'Mmm, Alan is Ian's brother, isn't that right? I'm looking forward to meeting him properly at Christmas. I met him very briefly in the shop recently when he was looking for Kirsty.'

'Mum, I know that look,' Lara said. 'I'd have thought that too, that Kirsty was interested in Alan, until yesterday. Now I'm not so sure. Until very recently he had a girlfriend. Maybe they got back together.'

'I hope not, for Kirsty's sake,' Martha sighed. 'I'd like to see her find someone special. I'm old-fashioned enough to be glad she's met him face to face and not over the internet.'

'Lots of people meet through the internet these days. I admit I was worried about Kirsty dating strangers, but I guess everyone is a stranger at first.'

'Very philosophical,' Martha said drily. 'However, usually it's a friend of a friend, or a friend's brother. That's the way we used to meet potential boy-friends. And yes, I know the world's moved on, so don't give me that pitying look, darling.'

Lara laughed. 'Okay, you win. Come on, let's take these costumes through to Moira. I think I can hear a break in the singing, so they'll be going through the drama now.'

★ ★ ★

'Will there be hot dogs, Miss Perfect?' William asked, fidgeting in the line at the back of the stage in his shepherd's cloak.

'What?' Lara was kneeling down and tying Lucy's shoelaces, which kept coming undone under her long white angel's dress. 'Straighten your halo; it's slipped again.'

She was too hot, her hair was coming loose from its bun, and tendrils hung in front of her eyes. The noise level was high, and the line of angels, shepherds and sheep was wriggling and jumping as thirty small children waited for the nativity to begin. Mary had been crying and her eyes were red. A sheep had stood on her toe. Lara had soothed her. Joseph had gone to the bathroom and she had to send a shepherd to get him.

'Hot dogs?' William shouted in her ear, his breath hot.

'Yes, there will be hot dogs after the show. And other nice food too. But not until we get this show on the road.' She clapped her hands smartly and the class stood to attention. 'Let's have hush.'

They put their fingers to their mouths quietly and Lara smiled, proud of them. Then they heard the piano starting up, and the audience of parents and carers and family members also hushed outside in the school hall.

'We're ready,' Lara said. 'Good luck, Primary One. It's going to be fantastic.' She pushed the three wise men gently through the heavy curtains and onto the stage. The Primary Five teacher ran up.

'Moira says you've to go and watch

the show. I'll take over directing. You deserve it. Go!'

Lara tiptoed into the darkened hall and saw an empty seat amongst the audience. She made her way to it and saw Ian. He smiled.

'I kept you a seat,' he whispered. 'Ms Mellon told me you'd be needing one.'

The three wise men were following a bright star. Lara leaned back in her chair, exhausted. Yet slowly she was drawn in to the magic of the ancient story, as she was every year. Ian took her hand as the shepherds herded onto the stage and William said his one-line speech. She didn't try to take her hand back. Ian's grip was warm and comforting. She thought of her mother and how she had denied there was anything between her and Ian. That was true, wasn't it?

She let her mind wander a little in the darkness. All around her, there was an atmosphere of love and happiness as families watched the nativity, enjoying their children's moment of fame or simply engaging with the drama and looking forward to Christmas.

She hadn't told Martha about the email Mark had sent. He wrote that he was leaving town. He had a new job somewhere, though he hadn't said where. He'd discovered through his final therapy class that Lara didn't deserve him. He advised her to get her own therapy. She had skimmed over much of this once she found out he was leaving for good. Reading that, she'd felt light, as if gravity no longer contained her. She had her life back. No more dreading the school gate or a late-night ring of her doorbell. But it was his last parting sentence that stuck with her. Mark hadn't liked Ian turning up to speak to him. He accused him of being in love with Lara and asked if she felt the same.

Lara had read that sentence twice before deleting Mark's email. She was not obliged to reply to him. In fact, she never needed to consider him again. Ever.

Was it true? Was Ian in love with her? Or was it another of Mark's exaggerations and jealousies? That was more likely. A flicker of disappointment. Lara suddenly realised that all her protestations were just that. She didn't want to be just friends with Ian. She wanted more. She wanted a chance to find out if there could be something special between them.

Was that even possible? How could it work, when Ian had William? She loved the little boy, and would never want to hurt him or confuse him by being together with his dad. Besides, she was his teacher. It was too complicated! And then there was Alicia, whose presence was tangible when Ian spoke about her. Lara couldn't compete with her.

She sighed in the darkness and Ian slid his shoulder in contact with hers as if to say, *I'm here*. She was touched by his gesture, even if he was the one making her sigh.

The nativity was in full swing. Mary

had dried her eyes and made everyone else's damp with her sweet voice as she lifted baby Jesus and showed him to all his worshippers. One of the sheep stumbled and nearly fell off the stage, only saved by the quick actions of the school caretaker, who was also their sound technician. Two shepherds had an argument about who was to stand in front of who. There was a small amount of shoving until the lead angel pulled her twin brother away.

None of these incidents spoiled the story, and some of them caused a ripple of amusement in the audience. There were plenty of flashes as cameras and phones captured the memories. Ian took many of William and showed Lara the pictures.

Then all too soon it was over, and everyone sang 'We Wish You a Merry Christmas' as a finale. Lara's palms were sore from clapping as the actors bowed and the piano teacher was presented with flowers. Then Lara and Moira were called up to the front and given colourful bouquets too.

She saw Ian grinning and applauding, and her mum doing the same and waving at the back. Moira got up on the stage and everyone quietened for the head teacher to speak. She made a short speech thanking everyone for their help and praising the young actors. After that, she proclaimed the winter festival open, and the Primary Seven pupils came in, dressed in black and white as waiters.

The audience stood up and made for the tables of food and drink at the back of the hall. Behind them, school pupils moved the chairs into casual groupings so people could mingle. William came running up to them, a hot dog dripping with ketchup in his fist.

'Wasn't it great? Did you see me?'

Ian laughed and ruffled his son's hair. 'You were amazing. Wasn't he, Lara?'

'You were amazing. You were all stars.' She found a clean tissue in her pocket and gave it to him. 'That's to mop up all that ketchup. It's gone inside your shirt cuff.'

Martha found them and they stood and chatted. Other parents came to say hello, and it became a very sociable afternoon. An hour later, full of cake and fizzy drinks, Lara was wilting a little. Ian pulled her aside.

'Do you fancy getting out of here?' he said. 'I heard from Moira that you're free to go. She said to tell you she expects you in tomorrow for a clear-up when school is shut. And your mother said to say goodbye. She'd have told you herself, but a group of the ladies are going on for coffee and she went with them.'

Lara smiled. Good for Martha. She was going to be okay. 'Yes, let's go. Where's William?'

'We'll pick him up on the way out. He's in the playground with some of the other boys. There's an ice rink set up in the town centre. Do you like ice skating?'

'I love it, but I'm not dressed for it.'

259

Lara glanced down at her skirt, tights and polished shoes.

'I'll drop you home and you can get changed.'

'You're not taking no for an answer, are you?' Lara smiled.

'This is the start of the holidays. Instead of New York, I've got this little town to play in, so I'm going to make the most of it.'

'Do you mind not going to New York?'

Ian shrugged. 'I'm over it now. I'll be honest — I was looking forward to a break somewhere different; but I don't care as long as I'm with my family. William didn't want to go since Uncle Simon's back from hospital, and we're looking forward to spending the day with your family.'

'How is your uncle?'

'He's improving but can be a bit grumpy. He didn't like the way we cleaned up his house while he was in hospital. He's insisted on putting back all the furniture and his piles of books everywhere. It's like an obstacle course. I'll be glad to move out.'

'Did you decide where you're moving to?' Lara said, swallowing a lump in her throat. She dreaded him telling her they were moving back down south.

'I still don't know yet, but it'll be somewhere around here. William is so settled at school that I don't want to move him again. Besides, I like it here.'

Their gazes caught. Lara thought how nice his hazel eyes were. She glanced away first, confused and flustered. They weren't leaving. Her heart sang.

★ ★ ★

The ice-skating rink had been brought in from the city by lorry and constructed in the town square. It was small but looked fun. They hired skates from a stall and sat on a row of benches to put them on. The square was busy now that school had finished up for the holidays. The shops were open and there were pop-up stalls too, selling spiced wine and ginger cakes and sausages.

'Can I have a sausage, Dad?' William asked as he pushed his feet into his skates.

'You can't still be hungry after that hot dog, surely?' Ian grinned.

William nodded. 'I had cakes too, but I've room in my tummy for more.'

'How about we skate first and then grab some food?' Lara suggested. She really didn't want to try walking across the square in her skates, now that they were firmly tied on.

She tied William's skates for him. They all walked carefully up the ramp to get onto the ice. Lara grabbed hold of the hand rail and slowly placed her skates onto the rink. She did love skating, but only did it once or twice in the year. It wasn't like riding a bicycle, she decided quickly, which was once learned and never forgotten. It was, at least for her, a skill that had to be learnt over and over again.

William skimmed across the ice like a natural. There was music playing, and coloured lights dappled the ice surface. There were other boys he knew, and soon he was skating in a group with them. Ian wasn't any more proficient than Lara.

'I thought, when you suggested skating, that you were an expert,' she panted, holding onto his arm for dear life as they made their tentative way across the end of the rink.

'I never claimed that. I like skating, but I've only ever done it a few times. Maybe I like the idea of it more than the real-life activity.' Ian clung to the handrail and helped her to it.

'It's fun, though,' she said. 'I'm enjoying myself. Aren't you?'

'Very much so,' he said.

They were tucked away at the back of the rink. William was making circles with his friends. Families and couples zoomed about on the ice. It was as if they were cocooned from the rest of the world. It seemed utterly natural for Ian to lean down and kiss her. Lara kept one hand on the handrail and reality while the other reached for Ian and the stars.

His kiss was warm and eager. Lara felt the beat of his heart over hers. When they broke free, they smiled at each other. Whatever it was, it was . . . *right*. Lara hoped that Alicia would approve, and somehow she thought she would. Her gaze turned to the rink, searching for William.

There he was. He'd stopped circling and was staring at them. He waved to Lara and then went back to his friends. Ian hugged her close. They had no need for words. They both knew this was the start of something real.

Lara felt a feathery touch on her cheek. Then another. A cry went up from the skating crowd and Ian laughed, pointing up to the sky. It was snowing.

15

Only a couple of days to go until the big day. The snow had been falling constantly for forty-eight hours, and the outside world was muffled in soft white. The snow sparkled under the street lights. Alan stared at it and then drew the curtains. He turned and swore under his breath as his shin bumped into a small table. Simon's home was back to normal. Everywhere there was a clutter of dark wood furniture, towering piles of newspapers and hardback books and eclectic objects such as a lone leather boot and an iron on the carpet.

He bent down to pick up the iron and then gave up. What was the point? Uncle Simon would have placed some other strange item there within minutes. Thank goodness he was moving out soon. Since the not-very-veiled hints from Simon that he wanted his home and gallery back and all to himself, Alan had searched the housing websites. He'd found a couple of properties that sounded interesting and had booked with the estate agencies to go and see them.

He didn't blame Simon in the least. His nephews had done their job of looking after his house and business, and he was right, it was time they moved on and into their own lives. Alan would miss the gallery. He'd enjoyed going there every morning early and preparing for the day. He'd enjoyed knowing that Kirsty was next door in her shop.

He wouldn't think about Kirsty. He'd messed that up. Since the disastrous kiss, he hadn't seen her. He'd kept out of her way, and he suspected she was avoiding him too. He sighed and shook his head. Then he glanced at his watch. Why was it, when one was at a loose end, that the seconds ticked by so slowly? It was five o'clock. He had driven Simon to the gallery that morning, under instructions, and left him there. There had been no offer for Alan to stay and help. Simon didn't want a lift home either. He was going to speak to Lisa and she'd drop him back. Alan wasn't needed. He was redundant.

He slouched down on the sofa and winced, dislodging the books from under the cushion and setting them down on the floor with the rest. He picked up the remote, intending to channel flick aimlessly.

The front door opened and shut. Alan put down the remote. Uncle Simon shuffled in, bringing a blast of cold air with him. The old man's nose was bright red and his eyes were streaming.

'Here, let me help you off with your coat,' Alan said, leaping up. 'Have a seat on the sofa and rest for a while.'

'I'm not an invalid, you know,' Simon said grumpily.

Alan noticed, though, that Simon didn't protest when he took his damp coat, or when he helped settle him onto the sofa cushions. He let out a rattling breath and coughed.

'Have you got a cold?' Alan asked.

Simon waved him away impatiently. 'You're hovering like a nursemaid. Away with you. I'm fine, I'm fine.'

'I'll get you a hot drink and then we'll make sure that you *are* fine,' Alan said firmly.

There was no protest at that, so he left Simon resting, made tea and brought it through. At first he thought his uncle had gone to sleep. He put the tray down carefully so that the porcelain wouldn't clink. Simon opened his eyes and brightened at the sight of the teapot and the plate of gingerbread. He rubbed his hands together.

'Thank you. Pour me a large one, would you?'

They sat and ate cake in silence. Upstairs, Ian was working in his room with the door shut. He hadn't wanted Alan's company that day either, despite Alan asking if he could help in any way.

It had been gently pointed out to him that he wasn't a trained architect and that Ian could easily do his own filing and phoning, but thanks anyway.

'Did Lisa give you a lift home?'

'Ah, Lisa.' Simon sniffed, then searched for his handkerchief and blew his nose loudly.

'Was there a problem?'

Alan drained his cup and took another slice of gingerbread. He slipped a slice onto Simon's plate too and pushed it towards him. Uncle Simon was looking too thin after his hospital stay.

'That woman can be extremely stubborn,' Simon said, frowning. 'I've known her a very long time, you know. Ever since she came to the town, in fact, and set up her café. She's never been one to mince her words.'

'What was she saying?'

'I was telling her that I don't want to buy her café. Instead of listening to me, she started talking about *your* plans for the gallery. Saying she thought it was a grand idea and that I should pay heed. I told her to put her café back on the market immediately. But she refused. She told me there's no urgency and she'd sooner I really mulled it over. Honestly!'

'I hope you haven't fallen out over it.'

Simon harrumphed. He peered over at Alan. 'You've never seen her in action, have you? She's like a tornado, that woman.'

Alan heard the note of admiration in Simon's voice.

'There'll be no hard feelings. There never are with Lisa,' Simon added with a chuckle. Then he stared at Alan. 'I haven't changed my mind. I'm not buying her café, whatever she says.' He pushed up from the sofa to stand, then groaned and clutched his side.

'Are you all right? Let me help you. What is it? Is there a pain?' Alan moved quickly to his side.

Simon brushed him away. 'It's nothing. I'm just a little tired. I'm going to my room for a nap.'

'I'm concerned about his health,' Alan said to Ian as they chopped vegetables for a stew an hour later.

'Do you think he's having a relapse? We should insist he goes to the GP tomorrow,' Ian said.

'I don't know what's wrong with him. He said he was tired, but I hope it's nothing worse. He's probably overdone it, working in the gallery today.'

'I'm surprised you didn't go with him.' Ian slid the pile of vegetables into the pot and made up the stock.

'He didn't want me there. I feel I'm not wanted anywhere right now.' Alan laid down the chopping knife on the bamboo board with a dull clunk.

'That was heartfelt. What's bothering you? You're not regretting leaving your job?'

'Heavens, no. That's the best decision I've made in a long while.'

'It's . . . it's not Karen, is it? Do you want to make it up with her?'

271

Ian's face was turned away so Alan couldn't read his expression, but he knew his little brother's feelings about Karen.

'I can put your mind at rest on that score. I don't want Karen back in my life.'

'So . . . ?'

Alan picked up the herbs and flung a large spoonful into the bubbling stew. Ian took the jar from him.

'So . . . I've been looking at houses to buy. I've found two I like and I'm going to view them soon.'

'That's good. I've been doing that too, browsing the websites. I'll wait until after the New Year before I look seriously. I'm staying in the town. It makes sense for William to go to the same school now he's made friends.'

Ian hummed a melody as he added the meat and a generous splash of red wine to the stew and turned the heat down to a simmer. Alan took a good long stare at his brother. There was something different about him.

'Why are you so happy?' he asked.

'It's not a crime, is it?' Ian said, with a big dopey grin.

'Spill the beans. In fact, you don't have to now. I've guessed. I'm happy for you, I really am.'

'She likes me too,' Ian said simply. 'I'm in love with Lara. I feel like the world is a different place.'

'That's wonderful.' He meant it too. He was pleased for Ian. He deserved his happiness after the terrible blow of losing Alicia and the struggle to bring up William on his own. 'What does William think?'

'He's happy. It's as if he knew all along it was going to happen and that it was meant to be. We've had a good chat, and he knows Lara won't replace his mother, but that he can have a second mum too.'

'He's a good kid.'

'Yeah, he is. So what's biting you?'

'I've been a fool. I've lost Kirsty's friendship.'

Ian raised an eyebrow. 'Are you

certain it's just friendship you're after?'

'I don't know. I thought . . . I told her I didn't want anything more so soon after Karen; but now that it looks like we've fallen out, I can't bear it.'

Ian tapped him on the shoulder. 'A little bird can tell me where Kirsty is going to be tonight. Want me to find out?'

★ ★ ★

Kirsty twirled in front of her mirror, then made a face. It was the Small Businesses Christmas party that evening, and she wanted to look her best. Not too casual but, not as if she'd tried too hard either. The cherry-pink flouncy dress wasn't cutting it. She unzipped it and stepped out of it, then put on her lime-green suit; it had a neat waisted jacket and a pencil-slim skirt. She pushed her hair up and imagined it in a French plait, but it was too harsh a look. She wasn't going to a networking meeting, for goodness sake.

She wandered into her kitchen, still dressed only in her bra and pants. She had, however, shaved her legs and painted her nails. A small victory there. She sat down in front of her open laptop with a sense of déjà vu. It was open at the home page of the Apple Blossom Dating website. It was so easy to reconnect to it. It was literally a click of the button, and she'd be right back where she started with her profile active and her messaging system ready to receive dates.

What did she have to lose? Nothing. That was the short and brutal answer. She was still cringing from seeing Alan. She'd told him she loved him. And what had he done? He'd run a million miles from her. He didn't love her. Not one bit. He was probably still in love with Karen and wanted her back.

Kirsty groaned. She was so embarrassed. Since that awkward kiss and her even-more-awkward confession, she'd avoided him like the proverbial plague. He hadn't been back into the shop or asked her to pop into the gallery for coffee, which had become a pleasant ritual. She missed him. But she had her pride. Her finger hesitated over the 'join' link.

She took her finger back and nibbled a nail absent-mindedly. Instead of rejoining the website for a date tonight, she could message Ben or Adrian directly. She didn't want to go on dates anymore; she just needed a partner for this evening. Whatever Alan felt about her, she couldn't switch off how she felt about him. She was in love with him, whether she wanted to be or not. So, no dates with other men. There was no point. But the invite to tonight's party was for two. It would be nice not to have to go in alone. Bella Smith never had that problem, she thought briefly. On the other hand, how many parties did Bella get to with a new baby to look after?

Kirsty smiled. It wasn't all bad being single. At least she had her independence. So what if there was no handsome cowboy to ride into town with her? She didn't need Alan or Ben or Adrian there. She would go to the party on her own. After all, it was the twenty-first century.

Emboldened by her own pep talk, Kirsty went back into her bedroom. She chose a simple black party dress and five-inch-heeled court shoes. She added a slim gold necklace and matching drop earrings. After some deliberation, she left her hair down, where it brushed against her shoulders. She stared in dismay at her nibbled nail polish and carefully repaired the damage, then allowed herself one final smile in the mirror for courage. Wrapped up warmly in a beautiful fake fur coat, she hurried out to get a taxi.

The party was already in full swing when she paid the driver and went up the broad steps to the venue. A gorgeous Georgian stone mansion had been hired for the evening. She'd been in it before for conferences and lunches. Tonight the red carpet had been rolled out, literally, at the entrance. She felt glamorous treading on it, as if she was going to the Oscars.

The doorman, complete with top hat and tails, bowed as she went by. Thank goodness she'd worn her high heels, new dress and furs. This was most definitely not a casual affair. She checked in her coat with a girl at the reception desk and put a bright smile on her face. It might not be a networking meeting, but no doubt she'd meet a lot of business people she knew.

Inside, the room was crowded with groups chatting and holding long-stemmed glasses of champagne. Everyone was dressed in their best. The air was hot with mingled perfumes and the heady scent of the ornamental lilies adorning the side tables. At the back of the long room, Kirsty spied a delicious buffet laid out. Her mouth watered. If there was to be no romance in her life, she'd take up eating as a sport.

She was hardly into the room when she was greeted by Lisa and Den, her husband.

'You look wonderful. Isn't this a marvellous party? Better than last year's by far,' Lisa shouted above the hubbub. 'Did you see that Simon's back running his gallery?'

'I didn't see anyone at the gallery today. I was run off my feet with the last of the shopping days before Christmas,' Kirsty called back.

Lisa beckoned her closer. Den threw Kirsty a look as if to say she shouldn't encourage his wife, then wandered off in the direction of the food.

'That's better; I don't have to bawl now,' Lisa said into Kirsty's ear. 'I noticed Simon's back in the gallery, but that nice young man, his nephew, had vanished today. What a pity. He was full of innovative ideas to modernise that place. Believe me, it needs it. Simon was running at a loss before his illness.'

'I didn't know that.' Kirsty was shocked. She didn't know Simon Timmons well enough to be his confidante, but she'd supposed he was doing okay. After all, there was always a good flow of people visiting the gallery.

Lisa nodded. 'Awful, I agree. He's such an old stick-in-the-mud.' She threw up her hands as if Kirsty had argued with her. 'Now, don't think I'm saying anything behind his back that I haven't said to his front. He knows my thoughts on the matter. If he doesn't change something soon, he won't have a gallery to putter about in. Which is what he's doing. He treats it as an extension of his home, but he needs a better business plan than that.'

'Maybe Alan can help him with that,' Kirsty said. 'He wanted to investigate buying your café to expand the gallery.'

'It's a fabulous idea, but Simon doesn't see it that way. I'm going to keep bullying him until he does. Alan, the nephew . . . he could be the breath of life that place needs.' Unexpectedly, she elbowed Kirsty sharply in the side. 'Speak of the devil. I must be off and find Den. Have fun.'

Kirsty turned round to see what Lisa had been staring at over her head. All the blood drained from her face and she felt quite faint. Her heartbeat picked up rapidly and her skin was prickly with awareness. Alan Carter was making his way towards her through the crowd.

She couldn't think of a single thing to say. She stood like an idiot, mouth open. Alan was dressed in a tux like most of the other men. His height, the breadth of his shoulders, his blue eyes and blond hair, all these burned onto her brain. She noticed other women noticing him. He didn't see them; he was staring straight at her.

'Hello,' he said.

'Hello,' she whispered, but she didn't think he'd heard her over the noise.

'Can we get out of here?' he said. 'I need to talk to you.'

* * *

For a man so desperate to talk to her, he hadn't said one thing since they left the venue. Kirsty was bundled up in her fur coat, glad of its warmth. Her heels crunched down on the fresh snow. Alan had led the way down the steps, Kirsty casting a rueful look at the last of the red carpet. They were now on the nearby cobbled lane next to the riverbank.

Alan stopped and leant against the rail, looking out at the inky black water. He didn't appear to feel the cold.

'Where did you get the tux?' Kirsty asked.

'It's Ian's. He found out from Lara where you were tonight and insisted I borrow his tux and go and find you.'

'Ian and Lara have their happy ending, or I should say, happy beginning. I'm really glad for them,' Kirsty said. She'd had a long sisterly phone call from Lara the night of the school show.

'Don't you want to know why I came to find you?'

She hunched inside her coat for comfort. The river was silent as it slid downstream like treacle in the street lighting, under the old stone bridge nearby.

'Oh, blast it,' he said and pulled her to him.

His lips were hot and urgent, melding to hers. She kissed him back just as passionately, holding nothing back. She wanted to stay there forever. To drift down the river with him, lost in his embrace, only the two of them in the universe.

Alan came up for air. He smiled down at her, his thumb tenderly smoothing her cheek.

'What was that for?' she whispered. 'You said . . . '

'Forget what I said the other day. I was a fool and I was scared.'

'A big man like you, scared?'

'We get as scared as small people, trust me,' Alan joked. Then his expression grew serious. 'I'm so sorry I ran off after you said you loved me. Do you love me?'

Kirsty opened her mouth but no words emerged. She couldn't say it again. Not if there was the slightest chance of rejection. It was all too painful, even while she dared to hope, seeing Alan's smile and the look he was giving her.

'Because, Kirsty Perfect, I am in love with you.' His voice was low and deep.

'Say that again.'

'You didn't hear me?'

'I might have caught part of it, I'm not sure. You have to say it again.'

'Only if you say it too.'

Kirsty allowed herself the pleasure of raising her mouth to touch his. This kiss lasted even longer.

'What changed your mind?' Kirsty said later, as they walked hand in hand along the riverbank lane.

'I couldn't imagine not seeing you anymore. You were avoiding me, and I was doing the same. No more popping in for coffee and a chat. No more being asked to mend your fuses in the shop. It was unbearable.'

'Well, I'm sure I can do my own fuses if necessary. I bought a book on DIY.

Actually, it's an extra present for Dad, but he's good at sharing.'

'You can come and fix any fuses in my new house.'

'You're moving out of Simon's?'

He put his arm around her and she felt the thrill of being a couple. *Of being in love*. She snuggled right in to him.

'I'm finding a place of my own. Simon's right, he needs his home back.'

'And the gallery?'

'I'm going to set up my own out of town somewhere. I'll miss being next door to you.'

'You have lots of plans.' She was suddenly lost, as if he'd left her.

'I want to share my plans with you. I'm not going back to being a lawyer. Does that upset you? I won't be your rich boyfriend, unfortunately.'

'Don't joke about that,' Kirsty said, holding his hand. 'I don't care if you're penniless. I love you.'

They walked a little more. Kirsty was chilled despite her coat, and the joy of being in love had made her hungry. 'Did you see the great buffet at the party?' she said.

'It looked very tasty. You want to go and get some of it?' Alan grinned.

'Do you mind? It's funny; I started the evening wanting a partner to go to the party with, and now I've got one.'

'Better make the most of it. You shall go to the ball, my darling.'

16

It was Christmas morning. William sat in his pyjamas next to the Christmas tree, playing with small gifts from his stocking. Father Christmas had been very generous, and there were toy cars, coloured pencils and a variety of chocolates and sweets spread out on the carpet in front of him.

On the sofa nearby, Ian sat watching his son and sipping strong, hot coffee. Alan got up and stretched. 'We're due over at the Perfects' for one-ish. I'd better start getting ready. It's been a very nice relaxed morning.'

William looked up. 'Do I have to have a shower today? After all, it's Christmas.'

Ian laughed. 'You still have to wash, even on Christmas Day. Anyway, you want to look your best for the party, don't you?'

William nodded reluctantly and went back to zooming his cars along a make-believe road.

'Any sign of Uncle Simon?' Alan said.

'He went off to get changed. You could check on him when you're going to your room. He seems more sprightly, what do you think?'

'Definitely. My guess is he simply overdid it on his first day back at the gallery. I don't think we need to worry about him going back to hospital.'

'Looking forward to seeing Kirsty this afternoon?' Ian asked innocently.

Alan reached over and mock-punched his brother's arm. 'As much as you're looking forward to seeing Lara.'

'Mmmm, that would be a lot, then.'

Both brothers grinned happily.

Alan bounded up the stairs. He didn't need Ian reminding him about Kirsty. He thought about her all the time. He couldn't believe they both felt the same way. He was in love with her and she was with him. All his doubts had fled. Kirsty Perfect really was perfect, in every single way.

He was about to go into his room when Simon appeared in his own doorway. He looked smart in a striped blazer and dark trousers, fresh crisp shirt and a tie. On closer inspection, the tie wasn't just red and green. It was a Christmas tie covered in tiny holly clusters. Kirsty would approve. Alan wondered if she'd be wearing her Christmas pudding dress for the celebration.

'Alan, have you got a moment? I need to talk to you.'

'Of course. What is it?'

'I don't want to say it in the hall. Come in here and have a seat.'

Simon indicated his room and went back inside. Alan followed him in. Simon was sitting on the edge of his bed. He pointed at the high-backed chair at the wall. Alan sat and waited. There was some huffing and puffing as Simon adjusted his position.

'I hope it's nothing serious?' Alan said.

'It is serious. It's about your future. And mine.'

'Right . . . '

'The thing is, Alan, I'm not getting any younger,' Simon said.

There wasn't much Alan could say to that without sounding rude. In fact, his uncle looked much better than he had done in ages. His colour was good and healthy, and there had been no repeat of the wincing and breathlessness of the day he'd been at the gallery. Alan had noticed his working hours were shorter. The gallery would be making less profit because of that, but it was no longer his problem. It was hard to stand back but it had to be done.

'I'm going to admit that I'm finding it difficult to keep the gallery open all day. I love being there, but I run out of steam halfway through the day.'

Alan didn't interrupt. He realised Simon had to get his speech out.

'Thing is . . . ' Simon went on, not

looking at Alan, ' . . . I could do with some help.'

Now, cautiously, Alan said, 'What sort of help would you want?'

Simon waved his hand vaguely. 'You know, someone to do the books, sell the art, organise guest artist displays and so on.'

'Quite a comprehensive list. You'll need someone with previous experience of running an art gallery.'

'Oh, let's stop beating about the bush. I'm asking you to come back and help a foolish old man who didn't know a good thing when he saw it. The gallery needs you, Alan. And so do I.'

Alan knew what it cost Simon in pride to say that.

'You're smiling like an idiot,' Simon said. 'So, what's it to be? Put me out of my misery.'

'It's a yes, Uncle Simon. It's a yes. Thank you.'

'I should be thanking you. Well, that's that sorted. We can thrash out the details after Christmas.'

Simon started to get up but Alan stopped him. 'That's not quite that. What about Lisa's offer?'

'Somehow I knew you were going to bring that up. I've already spoken to Lisa on the phone this morning.'

'And?' Alan said, hiding his dismay. Uncle Simon took stubbornness to a new level. Had he rebuffed Lisa for a final time?

'And, in light of me taking on an assistant, it makes sense to open up the gallery further. Perhaps offer light refreshments to our customers. Eh?'

'I'd like to give you a great big hug.' Alan grinned widely.

'That's going a bit far. But I accept your compliment. Am I allowed to get up now? You're not going to stop me and demand something else for the gallery?'

Alan shook his head. He went to the door. Just before he headed out to his own room, he leaned back in.

'Loving the tie. Happy Christmas, Uncle Simon.'

Kirsty and Lara were at their parents' house, helping Martha to prepare the Christmas lunch. The kitchen was warm and steamy and smelt of roasting turkey, herby stuffing and spices. Three glasses of mulled wine stood on the worktop, slices of orange and cloves floating on the top.

Kirsty was wearing her Christmas pudding dress. She teamed it with snowflake tights and put a snowman hairclip in her hair. Today was not for elegance, but for total indulgence in her favourite day of the year. Lara had gone for a more tasteful style. She wore a cashmere jersey dress in a soft caramel colour and comfortable sling-back shoes. Her hair was prettily tied back in a loose bun. To please Kirsty, the scrunchie was green, red and gold. Christmas colours.

Martha put out pans for the veg-etables and boiled the kettle for making the bread sauce. Lara knelt to retrieve the bowls and trays they'd need to put all the food in. Kirsty skipped over and got the mulled wine. She gave one to Lara and one to Martha.

'Let's have some of this before we get stuck into making lunch,' she said, raising her glass. 'This is to having the best Christmas ever. Right, Mum?'

'I'll do my best,' Martha said, taking a great big sip. 'How much sugar did you put in this?'

'Quite a bit. It balances out the cloves nicely, doesn't it?'

Martha took another exploratory sip and nodded. 'It gets better as it goes down.'

Kirsty noticed her mother's cheeks pink up. Lara looked rosy too. It was the heat in the kitchen, the excitement of the day and possibly the mulled wine taking effect. She certainly felt great, but that was Christmas. It never failed to delight. She hoped that was true for her mum too. She'd had such doubts about having the big day here in the new house. Kirsty kept her fingers crossed that inviting the Carters was a good idea after all.

'Where's Dad?' she asked.

'He took his glass of wine into the living room, ostensibly to tidy up. I'm not hearing much vacuuming though.'

'He's probably asleep,' Lara giggled. 'Remember last year when he snored all afternoon during the board games?'

There was a pause because that just brought back memories of Hambly.

'So, you were right, Mum,' Kirsty said loudly.

'About what?'

Both Martha and Lara stared at her, Hambly forgotten for the moment.

'Meeting a man. The online dating was rubbish. In the end, I met my perfect man in my shop. Imagine that.'

'Imagine that,' Martha echoed, smiling broadly and putting an arm round each daughter. 'It just goes to show that your mother always knows best.'

'Hey, I wouldn't go that far,' Kirsty teased.

'I'm very pleased that you're both so

happy. And I'm very glad that the dreadful Mark is out of the picture.'

'Yes; well done, Lara, for getting rid of him. That took a lot of backbone,' Kirsty said admiringly.

Lara blushed. 'I had help from Ian.'

'Yes, but it took guts for you to stand up to him and not keep meeting him,' Kirsty said. 'Did you say he was moving out of the country?'

'I got a final email from him,' Lara said. 'He says he's going to Africa to help build schools. It sounds very unlikely, but it must be true. He put a link on it to an overseas charity. I'm just greatly relieved he won't be around.'

'He's atoning for his awful behaviour towards you,' Kirsty said.

'Who knows . . . and who cares?' Martha said firmly. 'Now, more importantly, Kirsty, get another pan of mulled wine on the go for the visitors who will be here shortly. Lara, can you please check on the turkey? I'll go and wake Dad up.'

* * *

Their guests arrived promptly at one o'clock. There was a moment of awkwardness, as the hallway was so small it was difficult to greet everyone and move people into the living room. Kirsty saw Martha's unease before her mother put on a welcoming smile and guided them into the room. She hoped she hadn't made a mistake insisting on a Christmas at home. Lara had reminded them of Hambly. Would Bob and Martha have been happier this year celebrating in a restaurant?

Alan was last in the door. Kirsty kissed him. 'Happy Christmas. Isn't this great? Can you smell the turkey? You have to guess its weight. Mum bought the biggest one in the butcher's.'

'Happy Christmas, Kirsty Perfect. Is this the pudding dress? It's marvellous. I wish I'd worn something festive now.'

'You're looking pretty good.'

In fact, Kirsty thought he looked absolutely gorgeous in his charcoal trousers and blue shirt. She wanted to grab him and kiss him for hours. Which was entirely inappropriate, so she suggested they follow the others through instead.

'Actually, can we go somewhere a bit private for a few minutes?' Alan asked. He looked anxious.

'Is everything okay?' she asked, feeling as if his unease was infectious. What was wrong with him?

'Fine, fine. Where can we go?'

Behind them, in the living room, came the sounds of chat and laughter. Kirsty heard her father asking who'd like a drink, and the creak of furniture as they sat. They'd had to borrow an extra table to seat their guests for lunch, so there wasn't much space. No one seemed to care, though. Martha rushed through to the kitchen. There was a clatter of dishes. Lara followed with William, promising him they had fizzy drinks.

'Come on,' Kirsty said. 'Let's get out of the traffic. I can't be away too long though, as I'm supposed to be helping with lunch.'

'This won't take long,' he promised.

She led the way to the spare room. Martha had decorated it in pale lemon and lime-green. It was simply furnished with a double bed, wardrobe and a large standard lamp in one corner.

'Will this do?'

'It's quiet in here,' he said. 'It'll be fine.'

'What is it? Don't keep me in suspense. You do . . . you do still like me?'

'*Like* you?' Alan smiled. 'I love you, Kirsty. I like you too. You're my best friend and my best love all rolled up in one.'

'So . . . ?'

She was speechless when Alan got down on one knee. His hand trembled as he fumbled in his trouser pocket and brought out a small black satin box. 'Will you marry me? Please.'

Her heart thudded. She opened the box to see a diamond solitaire set in old gold.

'If you don't like it, I can take it back,' he stammered.

'Oh, Alan. I love it. But I love you more. Of course I'll marry you. Get up before you fall over.'

He got up and they embraced tightly. Kirsty felt their hearts beat in time as if they were one. That was how it was always going to be, she promised herself. They were two halves joined now forever.

'Shall we tell them our good news today? Or should we focus on Christmas and tell them tomorrow?' Alan said.

'I can't keep this a secret until tomorrow! No way. I want to see their expressions today. Christmas is always special, but now it'll be even more so. We'll remember this moment forever and each year, especially at this precise moment.'

'You are such a romantic,' Alan said, hugging her again.

They decided to wait until after Christmas dinner to tell everyone. The table was laden with festive food. Kirsty had decorated it with napkins and crackers. Each place had a small wrapped gift. These were wooden figures from the shop, a little memento of the day.

Bob brought in the turkey and they all applauded. He carved it expertly, and Martha distributed warmed plates for them to pile high with sausages, stuffing, sprouts, gravy and bread sauce. Simon had a paper hat on, after winning the cracker fight with William. Ian gave William his paper hat. Kirsty ruled that everyone had to wear one so that they all looked ridiculous.

Lara poured more wine and fizzy drinks. They laughed and groaned over the cracker jokes and had second helpings of the food. Just like every year, Kirsty thought it the best Christmas ever. Only this year it was true. She was engaged to Alan. She wished she could wear her ring, but she wasn't going to do that for another whole five minutes, when they'd announce their engagement to the family. Because now, all the people in this room were her extended family.

Ian rapped on the table for silence. 'Lara and I have something we'd like to tell you.'

They all turned to him.

'We're getting married.'

Kirsty was simultaneously delighted for them and annoyed that they'd beaten her and Alan to it. In the midst of all the congratulations, Alan rapped on the table, copying his brother. A host of questioning looks greeted him.

'Kirsty and I are getting married too.'

'Next Christmas,' Kirsty added.

'How about a double wedding?' Lara said. 'Mum, we'll need your help, and Dad, yours too. We want it to be the best wedding ever.'

The telephone rang in the hall. Bob got up to answer it. Whoever it was, it was a short call. He came back in and his eyes sought Martha's.

'That was the couple who bought Hambly. His job is being transferred to

Japan and they're putting Hambly back on the market. Very kindly, they wanted us to be the first to know. We can have first refusal on it.'

Martha looked around her. She watched her daughters with the men that they loved. She saw the table with its celebration meal. In the corner of the room, the Christmas tree lights twinkled with multicoloured splendour. Underneath the tree were the gifts waiting to be unwrapped. In the kitchen, the plum pudding was simmering gently in a pan of water. Soon it would be ready to be brought triumphantly in, set alight and then eaten with cream and brandy butter.

Bob was waiting. She knew how he felt. He was happy here. And she was glad to be able to put his mind at rest.

'I don't think so, do you? I'm very contented right here, and I'm already looking forward to a very special Perfect Christmas next year.'

We do hope that you have enjoyed reading this large print book.

Did you know that all of our titles are available for purchase?

We publish a wide range of high quality large print books including:
Romances, Mysteries, Classics
General Fiction
Non Fiction and Westerns

Special interest titles available in large print are:
The Little Oxford Dictionary
Music Book, Song Book
Hymn Book, Service Book

Also available from us courtesy of Oxford University Press:
Young Readers' Dictionary
(large print edition)
Young Readers' Thesaurus
(large print edition)

For further information or a free brochure, please contact us at:
Ulverscroft Large Print Books Ltd.,
The Green, Bradgate Road, Anstey,
Leicester, LE7 7FU, England.
Tel: (00 44) **0116 236 4325**
Fax: (00 44) **0116 234 0205**

LOVE ON TRACK

Jill Barry

Flora Petersen surprises family and friends when she successfully applies for a job as a train manager. Though nervous to begin with, she soon finds herself enjoying the daily routine of assisting passengers — including one she privately nicknames 'Mr Gorgeous'. Jack, father of a small daughter, commutes to his job via train. Since his wife died, he's had no time for romance. Until one day he notices the lovely woman who sells him a ticket, and realises he's seen her somewhere before . . .